Goodbye Tomorrow

Goodbye Tomorrow

Gryzelda Niziol Lachocki

Brunswick

Library of Congress Cataloging-in-Publication Data

Lachocki, Gryzelda Niziol, 1931–
    [Niezapomniane jutro. English]
    Goodbye tomorrow / Gryzelda Niziol Lachocki.
        p.   c.m.
    ISBN 1-55618-181-7 (alk. paper).
    ISBN 1-55618-183-3 (pbk. : alk. paper)
    1. Lachocki, Gryzelda Niziol, 1931-   . 2. World
War, 1939-1945—Deportations from Poland. 3.World
War, 1939-1945—Personal narratives, Polish.
4. Poles—Soviet Union Biography. 5. Refugees—
Poland Biography. 6. Polish Americans Biography.
I. Title.
D810.D5L2413   1999
808'. 066001—dc21   99-31949
                                          CIP

Published in the United States of America

by

Brunswick Publishing Corporation
1386 Lawrenceville Plank Road
Lawrenceville, Virginia 23868
1-800-336-7154

To the memory of the
Polish children who perished
in the Russian Labor Camps

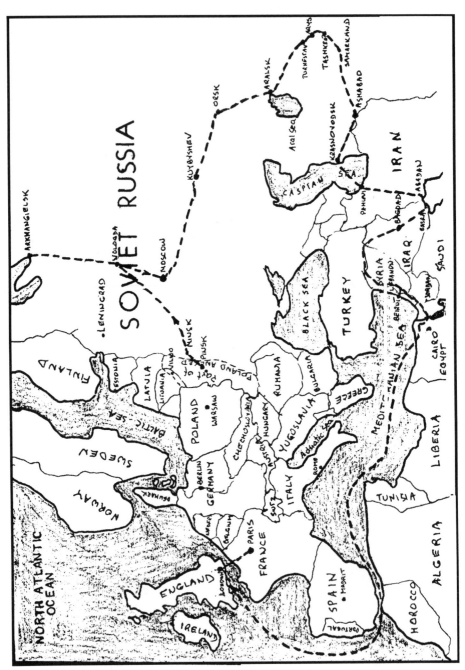

Author's road to exile and to freedom.

Table of Contents

Prologue

Since the seventeenth century, Siberia has been Russia's favorite place of correction and rehabilitation for enemies of the State. A mass banishment to Siberia occurred in 1863 after the January Uprising of Poland against the Russian invasion. Fifty thousand Poles were sent to Tomsk, Irkutsk, and Uhta in the north (Van Loons Geography, New York, Garden City, 1940). In Russian terminology these prisons were the places where, regardless of age, the enemies of Mother Russia were reeducated.

In 1939 Russia occupied more than half of Poland, which was inhabited by 13 million people. With the Russian invasion, the famed prisons of Vorkuta, Pechora, and Uhta were filled with Polish prisoners of war. Civilians were not spared either. They also had to be reeducated. The first large transport to Siberia on February 10, 1940, was composed of farm owners, no matter how little land they had. This convoy of 110 trains with 2,000 civilians in each, 220,000 total, was sent to northern Siberia. The second transport in April 1940 carried 320,000 Poles on 160 trains, to the Republic of Kazakhstan in central Asia. The Kazakhstan Republic encompasses an area larger than India.

Stalin's philosophy was to scatter Poles all over Russia, not too many in one region, so they would either perish from hard work and starvation, or, if they survived, be integrated into the local population.

Between 1939 and 1941, Russia deported one million and 680,000 Polish citizens to Siberia. Prisoners of war were not included in this number. Among the deportees was a small group of Ukrainians, Belorussians, and Jews.

The deportation of civilians never really ceased, although it was not always on such a large scale. It continued through 1945. By 1942 one third of the deportees had died. Mainly, the oldest and the youngest (Sikorski Institute, London).

The author was born in a small village in the eastern part of Poland. The quiet, bucolic life of the region was interrupted by the Second World War. The author, with her family, was deported to Russia and spent two years in the Russian labor camp near Archangel in northern Siberia.

After the amnesty she left Russia, traveled through Asia, Africa, and the Mediterranean Sea to England where she married an electronic engineer and immigrated to the United States.

This personal tale of triumph of the human spirit in the face of nearly incomprehensible tragedy and tyranny encompasses an amazing wealth of experience and material. The will of the Niziol family to stay together and survive exile, Siberia, and uncountable dangers was full of courage and triumph. Throughout the entire ordeal there was optimism, even with death looming everywhere, and one has to believe that it was this steadfastness of heart that got the Niziols through.

CHAPTER ONE

Childhood

Written memories,

Hidden emotions revealed,

Soul nakedness.

It was only the beginning of June in 1937, but the heat was suffocating. The trees with their droopy leaves stood silent, and the grass was yellow. Small lizards played on the wall of the barn. In the house with a thatched roof, three children lay on their beds sick with dysentery. The little boy, youngest in the family and the only boy, was only one year old. Josephine was three, and I (Gryzelda) was five. Our mother was worried sick that we might die. She worried even more because her babies were not baptized.

The four older girls in this family were baptized before they reached their first birthday, but, when I was born, our old priest had died, and our Catholic practices stopped. We had a very young priest. My father had an unresolved conflict with young priests dating to his youth. My father was only twelve years old when his parents died. He became the head of a household with a younger sister and a brother.

At the turn of the century, Poland as a nation didn't exist, and my father lived under Russian occupation. People were persecuted and discouraged from Catholic practices. They were even forced to change their religion to Russian Orthodox. Very often priests cooperated with Russian officials, and, when my father wanted a funeral service in church, the young priest demanded some money. Since my father didn't have any, the body of his father stayed at home for an entire month until neighbors contributed funds for the funeral. After that, my father had a physical and spiritual aversion to young priests.

I, and my younger sister and brother were sick, and my mother decided that she would do everything to have us baptized. She begged, pleaded, and threatened, and it was only after reminding Father that Thad was the only son, who soon might be the dead son, that Father relented. All three of us lay on a farmer's cart, and this way we went to our church in Lahishyn, which was about seven kilometers away.

At the church, everything was ready. My mother carried Thad; Josephine and I walked. The priest started with Thad, then Josephine, but when he heard my name, he refused to baptize me, because it was not a saint's name. That angered my father. He grabbed all three of us and we went home. My mother cried all the way.

After one week, Josephine and I felt a little better, but Thad was getting worse. I was really glad that we were not baptized, because I didn't like the name Josephine. I wanted my sister to be Kay instead of Josephine. I begged my mother to return to the church to change Josephine's name to Kay. I was pestering her, and finally she said, "If you like this name that much, we will give it to you." As much as I had liked the name Kay before, I now hated it and never used it. In time I dropped it.

Thad was seriously ill. We went back to church and this time we were baptized: Thad, Josephine, and Kay-Gryzelda. If Thad had been a girl, my father would have had us dead rather than ask that young priest to baptize us. After baptism we stopped at the doctor's office and obtained some medicine. In a few days Thad felt better, and life became normal. Our father had wanted all of us to be boys because he needed help on the farm. Unfortunately he had to contend with girls.

Thad, growing up among girls, didn't want to look any different. Reluctantly, he wore shorts, and tried to do everything we did. He had long blond hair.

During the First World War, my father was old enough to enlist in the army. When Poland regained independence in 1918, my father was a police officer in the Warsaw district where he met my mother. They married in 1921 and a year later their first daughter, Bronica, was born in Warsaw and baptized in St. John's Cathedral. As a reward for his military service, Father received thirty hectares in the eastern part of Poland, in the district called Polesie.

The greater part of Polesie was forest full of wild animals, wetlands, fish-filled rivers, and meadows fertile with hay. The largest city was Brest (Brzesc), the capital. Pinsk was our county seat and Lahishyn our nearest town, where all the children from adjacent villages completed their elementary education.

In Lahishyn we had Catholic and Orthodox churches, also Catholic and Orthodox cemeteries. Those two churches were in continuous, friendly war. Catholics claimed that Orthodox clergy stole the picture of Mary from the Catholic Church. The Orthodox claimed that the Tsar had given it to them when he closed the Catholic Church during the occupation.

The Icon appeared in the Orthodox Church on certain

occasions, and at other times in the main altar in the Catholic Church. We never knew who made the switch, and the truth was always biased.

With the help of in-laws, my father cleared off some trees, built a house, a byre, barn, and started farming. There was much grazing land, some forest, and arable land for potatoes, rye, vegetables, and fruit trees.

Since Polesie had many wetlands, it was a mosquito haven. Bronica was bitten by a malarial type and was very sick. The doctor told our mother to send Bronica away to a better climate; otherwise, she would die. Maternal grandparents who lived at the outskirts of Warsaw took care of Bronica until she was eight.

Our village, Martynowka, had eleven families who had received their land after military service. There were also other families who had lived there for generations. All the farmers worked without interfering with each other, and there was relative harmony. All children attended the same elementary school, which was in the next village inhabited by Belorussians. There were only four grades in that school. To get there, we had to cross the bridge over the Canal Oginski. This canal was a vital waterway. It connected the Baltic Sea through the Bug River with the Black Sea through the river Dnieper. Originally, all these villages had belonged to Count Oginski. The Count was fondly remembered by those who knew him. He was also a composer and his "Polonaise" is still a famous piece of music.

The school had a Polish teacher, and everybody studied the Polish language, history, and mathematics. Religion was taught in both, Polish and Belorussian languages. Because of religious tolerance, it was considered in the national interests to allow each ethnic group to study its religion in its own language.

There was one radio in school. Once, the teacher took us for a visit to his friend's home, where there was a piano. This was a rare treat. The teacher wanted to enrich our environment and our culture. After the fourth grade, most of the children went to Lahishyn, our nearest town, where they attended school until the seventh grade. For most of the children this was the end of their education. They had learned how to read and write, the rudiments of arithmetic, geography, and history, and a great many things about farming. At the age of fifteen, children assumed many adult responsibilities.

When Bronica was eight years old, my grandparents decided it was time for her to get to know her own family. They brought her to us, and after a short visit, the grandparents returned home. Bronica thought that she had came only for a visit and was ready to go back. With horror, she learned that this was to be her home, and that those four girls were her younger sisters. She cried, and called her mother "Ma'am" and her father "Mister." She didn't want to have anything to do with her parents or sisters.

At her grandmother's house, she had been the youngest, and everybody had taken care of her. Here, she had to take care of her sisters and help her mother. She cried herself to sleep every night. If she had been older, she would have run away from home. After many months she reconciled herself, accepted her parents, and even had some fun with her sisters.

For Bronica, time seemed to rush by. After fourth grade, she went to Lahishyn to continue her schooling. She walked the seven kilometers to Lahishyn every day. During the winter, she boarded in town with a family. By the time she finished the seventh grade, our family had seven children, six girls and a boy, the youngest. Bronica had to assume the role of a grown boy, and every day worked with Father in the fields. As our father's health failed, she had to do more and more. He had suffered wounds to his lungs during the war, was a very heavy smoker, and developed cancer of the lungs.

There were many young people in our village. When they were not in school or working in the fields, they went swimming and canoeing, they picked mushrooms and berries, and sometimes had barn dances. Very often, the villagers met in somebody's barn for story-telling. Usually the stories were of the last war or about the famine, how whole villages and towns had starved to death. Some desperate parents had killed their children and committed suicide. These were frightening stories, and long into the night after I heard them, they kept me awake. Very often somebody brought a book to the barn and read aloud while the rest were busy with their tasks. Women and girls crocheted, embroidered, spun, and wove baskets, men repaired the harness, and boys tried to fix farm equipment. The evening ended with the singing of popular or religious songs. These gatherings lasted well into the night. People worked hard, but they also enjoyed each other's company.

My mother came from a family of nine children: three girls and six boys. All the boys in the family received higher education. The girls on the other hand, were taught at home by their brothers. Only the youngest sister graduated from high school. My mother was the second oldest child and very early had to take care of her brothers and sisters.

In the spring of 1938, my mother's youngest sister, together with her girlfriend, came for a visit. There was so much excitement not only in our house but also in the whole village. We considered our guests very sophisticated. Both were high school graduates. They were in their twenties, and they came by train from Warsaw, a distance of four hundred kilometers. As far as we were concerned, Warsaw was probably at the end of the earth. When they arrived, our house was full of the village children. They all wanted to see the new arrivals. Everybody invited us to visit them, and bring our visitors with us.

We wanted to show our visitors how we lived. On the first morning, barefoot, we took them into the woods. Not only did we show them the nests of wild birds, but we also picked berries and waded through ponds to gather water lilies. The two young women were petrified. They screamed at the sound of branches cracking under our feet, saw shadows behind every tree, and avoided the pond. We scared a snake out of the grass, and that made them run for their lives. We had more in mind for them.

Since it was hot, we decided that all of us would sleep in the barn at night on the straw. We told unbelievable stories of snakes that were found under the covers, large jumping frogs, and spiders. These stories gave the visitors quite a few sleepless nights, but they gradually realized that despite all those horrors, nothing bad had ever happened to us. They learned to listen to our stories with great skepticism. Soon, they were running barefoot with us, and even porcupines didn't frighten them. In this bucolic setting they spent the whole month and started calling themselves country girls. They insisted that they had a wonderful time.

Bronica received from the visitors a beautiful white dress dotted with blue pansies. The dress was so special to her that she wore it only to church or to a dance with her boyfriend, Walter. Walter was nineteen. He worked as a riverboat sailor maintaining the sluices on the canal. He lived in Pinsk, which was twenty-five kilometers away. Sometimes he would ride his bicycle from Pinsk.

Bronica loved her white dress and took very good care of

it. She washed it gently by hand and hung it on the line to dry. It happened that one day a pig was out of his pen, got hold of the dress, and ripped it to pieces. Bronica was outraged and ready to kill the pig. She had lost the beautiful thing she cherished.

A young man, Jozef Bednarczyk, tried to capture Bronica's attention. He lived nearby, and tried to visit Bronica often, but she didn't pay much attention to him and discouraged his wooing. She preferred Walter, who was a gentleman, handsome, and fun to be with, while Jozef always talked about his ideas of Communism, how great it would be if only people would embrace this new philosophy. At sixteen, Bronica was bored by politics and Jozef.

When my mother married, her father had given her some land. She left it with him to use it as he wanted, and he paid her a yearly stipend. Since now our father was ill we needed the money to buy a horse, and we also needed to get some farm help. Our mother went to visit her family and she asked for more aid. One of her aunts, Zandara, was very rich. She had a food store in the center of Warsaw. Her house was filled with great art. Her two sons were educated in Germany and were art dealers.

The aunt, Zandara, in addition to being rich and highly educated, was very generous and gave mother some money and many gifts for the whole family. She also sent many toys for the children. My father received a beautiful coat. It became a source of envy for our neighbor, named Obara.

The village needed a bailiff and my father wanted this position. Obara came to our house and said to my father: "The villagers agreed to meet in my house to elect a bailiff. Please come tomorrow, in the evening, at seven."

The next day, my father dressed in his new suit and coat because he wanted to impress the villagers. He was after their votes. He went to Obara's house. The door was open, so he went in and was very surprised to see the empty room.

"Where is everybody?" he asked, but Obara didn't answer.

"Come right in," Mrs. Obara broke the silence. "Have a seat."

Father didn't bother to take off his coat, and sat on the bench by the table. "Where is everybody?" he asked again.

"The villagers were not interested in the bailiff position, so they refused to come," Obara answered. "We can settle this between ourselves."

"Wait a moment. The bailiff is supposed to be elected by all the villagers, not by just the two of us," said Father.

"It doesn't matter. They will accept what we will decide."

"I respect our neighbors, and I would feel very bad without their participation," Father insisted.

"I told you, we can settle it all between us," said Obara.

Father was angry and started to leave.

"Wait, let us have a neighborly talk," said Obara, holding my father by the hand.

Father sat back reluctantly, not wanting to leave in anger.

"Your wife bought so many beautiful things for your family. She must have spent a lot of money." Obara continued.

"Her family is very generous. They have sent us many gifts."

"Surely they also sent you money," insisted Obara.

"The money they sent is for our needs. We need it very badly because we have to buy a horse. Our old horse can't work anymore."

"I would like to ask you to lend me one hundred zloty."

"It is out of the question. I don't have any money to lend. Did you ask me to come to your house under the pretext of the meeting so you could weasel some money out of me?" Father became very angry and started walking toward the door. Obara and his wife were furious. They tried to block the way. When Father pushed Obara aside, she flailed at him with an ax and hit him over the head and shoulders. Father managed to escape. Under the darkness of the night he arrived home with a blood-soaked coat and his head mutilated.

My mother opened the door. The figure she saw petrified her. She didn't recognize her own husband. "Bronica, come see who is at the door!"

Father tried to talk but his words were garbled. Finally, Bronica recognized our father and pulled him in. They washed off his blood and rushed him to the hospital. He stayed in the hospital for two weeks. Though not fully recovered, he came home to take care of the farm. Mother filed a complaint with the police, but Obara disappeared.

Our father's health deteriorated. At sixteen, Bronica assumed responsibility for the whole farm. My second sister, Ema, who had just finished seventh grade, worked with Bronica. Michalina and Helena were still in school in Lahishyn. I, the fifth one, had just started the first grade, and had to take care of Josephine and Thad. We all did what we could, and somehow everything was done.

At the end of June 1938, our father died. His funeral was the saddest day of my life. Only three people—my mother, Bronica, and our neighbor, Ignalo—escorted his coffin on a one-horse driven cart to Lahishyn. The rest of the family never got a chance to see Father's grave. After our father's death, our neighbors tried to help us, but they had their own farms to take care of and were convinced that, without the head of the house, we would all die of starvation.

When harvest time came, Bronica took charge of cutting the grain, digging out potatoes, gathering the vegetables, and taking care of our animals. Since we had much grazing land, we took cattle from other farms to fatten them up. They grazed from frost to frost. Our mother had to milk them and do with the milk whatever she could. We always had plenty of milk, cheese, and butter. There was plenty of food, a roof over the head and enough clothing to cover our bodies.

When Father had been alive, he bought chickens in the surrounding villages and we shipped them to Warsaw, where my mother's aunt had a food store. We always hired some help. Hired men would come at sun-rise with their scythes, hone them, and work in the fields. The sound of honing the scythes had much promise in it. I loved to listen to it. But, after our father's death, all this work had to be done by hand. The cows, the vegetable garden, and the house kept mother busy all day long. All the work in the field was Bronica's responsibility. There was no money to hire anybody, so the whole family, from sunrise to sunset, cut grain and hay for the animals for winter. After the grain was cut and dried, it had to be hauled into the barn, threshed, and stored for the winter. Potatoes had to be dug, and, again, the whole family worked the rows. I would take Josephine and Thad and tend the cattle.

Thad, being only two years old, got tired very quickly and would fall asleep under a tree or in a furrow. Later, Josephine and I would have to go and look for him.

After we gathered the grain and potatoes, we made hay stacks. Then was time to start plowing the field for the next year's grain. Bronica plowed the field all day long with the reins on her neck, but the bridle made so many blisters on her neck that the next day she asked for help. After that, while she plowed, Ema held the reins. Working together, they finished plowing and harrowing the field while mother sowed the seeds. During the winter, after we had threshed the grain, Bronica took it to the mill and brought back flour.

In spite of their tender ages, Bronica and Ema worked from sunrise to sunset. At noon, Michalina or Helena would bring them something to eat. They sat in the shade of a tree, rested a little while eating, and went right back to work. They didn't complain because they knew that the life of the entire family depended on them. My mother considered Bronica and Ema partners and expected them to work as hard as she did. The girls only occasionally allowed themselves, after work, the luxury of a swim in the canal.

A year had passed since father died. It seemed that we had a hold on our future.

CHAPTER TWO

September 1939 (WWII)

Red sky, horizons,

Winter of mind and soul,

Night locked in blackness.

I t was September 1, 1939, the first day of school. I loved
school and could hardly wait for the school year to
begin. I was about to start the third grade and Josephine
was about to begin her first. We were both walking along
the road picking wild flowers to take to our classrooms.
When we reached the bridge over the canal, we met
Belorussian men who busied themselves as if they were
going to dismantle the bridge. They did not let us pass.

"Go home. The school is closed."

We stood there wondering what they were talking about.

"There is a war. Germany invaded Poland. Soon our
brothers will come from the east and everything will be all
right."

We ran home with this news, marveling at the number
of their brothers and wondering what they were bringing
with them to make everything all right. Later our sisters
returned from Lahishyn with similar news.

When our parents moved to this village, they had been happy that it was so far away from everything. They were sure that it was the most remote and peaceful place and they could forget all about wars. Now, our little village saw many people wandering from house to house asking for food and a place to rest. We had little food ourselves but we let them stay in our barn as long as they needed.

In fear of local Communists who had already robbed a few farmers, we had to hide some grain for the next year. We filled three grain boxes with the grain. The family went out to look for a safe place to hide the boxes. We found a place that we considered suitable, dug the holes, lowered our boxes, and covered them with straw and dirt. Our mother warned us, "Never come to this place or tell anybody about it."

Every day more and more people passed through our village and frightened us with their stories. Most of the people were women and children. They were running away from the Germans and had no special destination. They had lost their homes and carried their sparse belongings. Lucky were those who had a horse and a cart. Most of them just walked; dazed and haunted by their tragedy.

Fall arrived in its full glory. The leaves changed their colors to golden, rust, red, and brown. I especially loved the aspen leaves. They were very colorful and seemed to shiver. Now in this angry chaos of war the slight shivering increased. Shaken by the roar of German planes the leaves dropped to the ground and, with the next gust of wind, soared up again as though they were seeking a place to hide. Wild flowers bloomed profusely as if they were saying that it would all pass.

I remember I saw a plane one day as I was playing in the field. I waved and jumped up and down with joy, admiring this steel bird. Now German planes were flying so low and the pilots with their ugly swastikas looked so savage that everybody ran for cover. Our fears were palpable and real. Often the pilots shot anything that moved, including animals and young herdsmen.

Salt, sugar and kerosene, were vital items on the farm. Now it was impossible to get any of them. At night, the only light in the house was from the kitchen stove. We tried to finish everything before dark. Mother locked the house and in its darkness we sat quietly, or sang religious songs to lift our spirits and ask for God's protection.

Two weeks after the German invasion, "brothers" came. Local Communists started liberating us. They liberated us from our horses and all the hay we had stored for our animals. Jozef Bednarczyk, one of the local boys who had an eye for Bronica, revealed himself as a dedicated Communist and became the Communist mouthpiece. He ran from house to house and shouted that the front was going to pass through the village. In the evening all the men and older boys were arrested and we heard shooting in the distance. All the people in the village were terrified and confused.

My mother killed twenty chickens, put them in a sack, gathered all of us on a cart, and we went to one of our neighbors' homes. Many other villagers were there. As we carried the sack full of dead chickens, their blood marked the path behind us. I don't know why she killed them but in all the confusion she felt the meat would sustain us for a while. We forgot to pack a cooking pot and other utensils.

More and more villagers were coming to this house. Tired children cried. The owners of the house were desperate and frightened. "Why did you come here? Go away! Wait, don't go, stay, so we can all be killed together. Maybe if they see so many of us, they won't kill us."

Some of the neighbors left their homes open and let the

animals out in the fields. After a while, they left the children on carts and went back to look for their animals. Children were crying, dogs were howling, and there were loud rifle shots near the village. The night sky was red with fires. Fear gripped everybody and paralyzed their senses. Young boys kept watch, but courage was not their forte and every few minutes they would run back asking how soon all this would end.

Zygmunt was one of the villagers. In all the confusion he was the only one who could think straight. He tried to calm everybody and said that he would take care of us. Zygmunt was blind from birth but he had no problem getting where he wanted. He knew everybody in the village by name and where they lived, and could recognize them by their voices. He was trusted with the care of the frightened women and children. He didn't need any light to walk during the night. It was his moment of greatness and he took advantage of his abilities. He went to investigate where the shooting was coming from and why.

Between the village and the marshes, there was a piece of wasteland called the dogs' cemetery and that is where the shooting occurred. When Zygmunt reached the place he became aware of many people. He recognized the voices of arrested villagers and heard someone playing the violin. Zygmunt also heard the voice of Jozef Bednarczyk who screamed and cursed the arrested men, blaming them for all the trouble in the world. Later, Zygmunt heard screams and shots. By morning everything was quiet. He brought this news to us. The next day, one of the boys named Janek confirmed Zygmunt's words. Janek's father was Obara, the one who had attacked my father.

When the Communists had came to arrest Obara, they couldn't find him, so they had blindfolded Janek, his son, taken him to the dogs' cemetery, and said, "Play your violin as loud as you can and do not stop." Janek played while they were shooting villagers one by one. One week later the families were notified that all arrested men and boys had been shot and buried in the dogs' cemetery.

Ignalo, our nearest neighbor, who helped us when our father was ill, was also arrested. His wife, Natasha, who was pregnant with their fifth child, was told by a local Communist, "We can free your husband, but he will cost you money." She took all the money she had and went to Pozecze where her husband was imprisoned. Before she left, she brought her children to us, and they stayed with us for the whole week when their mother was away. She paid the money and came home. Ignalo was going to be released the next day.

Two days passed and there was no sign of Ignalo. Natasha went back.

"I paid you all the money you requested so where is my husband?"

"We were about to release him yesterday, but he tried to escape, so he was shot."

Desperate and broken, Natasha begged the Communists to let her know where her husband was buried. She wanted to give him a proper burial. She had to sell a cow for a bribe. They showed her his grave and told her, "You can dig him out if somebody will help you."

Natasha came to my mother begging for help.

"Help me to dig up Ignalo's body, so I can give him a proper burial."

Ignalo was a very good neighbor and had helped us a great deal when my father was sick.

"What will happen if they kill us both?" my mother cried. "You have small children, and I have small children. Who will take care of them? I think it really doesn't matter to a dead person where he is buried. Maybe we can call a priest and he could say burial prayers over the grave, and that would ease your mind."

"I don't want my husband to be buried by the road like a dog. Please help me, I have no one else to go to."

They both cried and thought that maybe Bronica could help.

"Bronica, help me. You are young and strong. I know you are frightened, but you are young, and you will get over this bad experience." Natasha begged and begged.

Bronica was also very frightened. She could be killed too, and how was our mother going to manage without her? Bronica was also deathly afraid of corpses. Natasha dropped to her knees, cried, and begged. My mother and Natasha begged. Bronica, in tears, reluctantly consented. With Natasha, they harnessed the cart, took shovels, ropes, and went to the designated place.

It was afternoon when they found Ignalo's grave by the road near the forest. They started digging. Both of them were afraid that the people who killed Ignalo and other men might come out from the forest and kill them. The deeper they dug, the less Natasha could help, and so Bronica did most of the work. By the time she reached the cadaver, she was so deep that only her head was above the hole. "Why would the murderers bury him so deeply?" She cried from fear and from the possibility of being buried alive. This fear of dead men and deep holes remained with her for the rest of her life.

Bronica tried to tie the ropes around Ignalo, and to lift him above her head. Natasha pulled, Bronica lifted, and after an extreme effort, the body was out of the hole. Together, they laid him on the cart and went home.

Looking at her husband's body, Natasha concluded that it was impossible for him to escape. His hands and legs were tied and Ignalo had received a severe beating before he was shot. His face was cut in strips, and the rest of his body had many wounds. Bronica went to Lahishyn to arrange for the funeral and to buy the coffin. Natasha's baby was born during the night, and my mother attended as midwife. My mother and Bronica had to take care of us, Natasha's children, and all of our combined animals. At the funeral Natasha, supported by Bronica and a few other neighbors, walked all seven kilometers to Lahishyn where Ignalo was buried.

One morning Bronica took all of us into the woods to gather wood for fuel. Our mother was home alone when she noticed a shadow at the door. When she looked up, she saw Obara. He looked disheveled. His clothes were dirty and shabby. My mother felt pity and contempt. "How dare you come here?"

"Please, don't scream," Obara whispered in a harsh voice. "A band of Communists are after me. You have to hide me. This is the last place anybody would expect me to come."

This was our mother's chance to take revenge for all the suffering he had caused us. Yet the noise of the approaching band convinced her that she must hide him. Otherwise, both of them might be killed.

"Run to the barn and hide behind the straw and sacks of grain."

Soon, the band of young Communists arrived with pitch forks, scythes, and wooden sticks to confront our mother.

"Give us all the arms you have. Where did you hide Obara?"

"This is the only weapon I have." She showed them a broom. "As for Obara, you can look all you want."

They looked through the house and the barn and left.

When we came home, our mother told us about what had

happened. She didn't tell us that Obara was hiding in the barn for fear that one of us might betray him. During the night Mother gave him some bread and the address of her family near Warsaw. In the morning Obara was gone. Before Christmas we received a parcel from our mother's family. The package had some kerosene, sugar, and salt. We also received a little note in the package telling us that the "sack of grain from your barn arrived safely."

One evening soon after that, Bronica had finished her chores and had gone to get wood for the fireplace, when in the distance she noticed a horse-drawn cart coming toward her. She recognized the rider as Jozef Bednarczyk and was petrified. She remembered what Zygmunt had said of Jozef's activities during the shooting of the villagers, and she suspected Jozef of shooting Ignalo.

Jozef greeted her as if he were her best friend. "I have a very good news for you, Bronica," he said, smiling.

Petrified, Bronica stood there silently.

"You are invited to a dance in Lahiszyn, and I came to pick you up. Put on the best clothes you have. I will wait for you."

"It is late, it is in the middle of the week, and I have a lot of work to do. Besides, I don't have any nice clothes. I don't want to go to the dance and I don't want to go with you!"

"I won't take no for an answer. I have promised the commandant that I will bring you. The Russians are our friends and we can not disappoint them. Get dressed and let us go."

"I told you I don't want to go."

"I was asking you politely, but you didn't understand. You have no choice. I came to take you whether you like it or not."

"If you are taking me by force, then you have to take me the way I am."

It was a cold day, and Bronica wore her father's long boots all muddied up, his coat, and a woolen kerchief on her head. She worked in the barn and had to keep warm.

"Let me tell my mother."

Bronica told Mother about Jozef's demand, and both of them were very worried. Mother warned Bronica not to go, but Jozef insisted that they had to go at once. Reluctantly, Bronica got on his cart, and they rode in complete silence.

The closer they got to Lahiszyn the greater fear gripped Bronica. When they reached the outskirts of the town not a single light was visible. The town looked dead. Jozef directed his horse to one of the buildings and stopped in front of the commandant's house. Bronica was panic-stricken. Jozef got off the cart and pulled Bronica off. He knocked at a door, which was opened by a soldier, and requested to talk to the commandant.

The commandant was a man in his early forties, with a handsome face and with sad, dark eyes. He looked at Jozef with a hint of recognition and asked the purpose of his visit. Jozef dragged Bronica and pushed her toward the commandant.

"We are so grateful for all the help you brought us that I am giving her to you, so you can sleep with her."

The commandant looked hurt and annoyed. He pulled Bronica to the light, looked at her face, which at this moment had the expression of a cadaver, and turning to Jozef said: "I have a daughter at home her age. You are going to take this young woman home, and if anything happens to her, I will hold you responsible, and she better be all right." He turned to Bronica.

"If he mistreats you, come and tell me about it."

Jozef obediently took his seat on the cart. The commandant helped Bronica back into the cart and hit the horse to make it go. Bronica felt grateful to the commandant but was terribly hurt. Her hurt was so great that, without tears, she sobbed all the way home like a beaten dog.

"How could you do thing like that to me? We grew up together. Don't you have any conscience?"

"The most important thing for me is to be a good Communist, and nothing will stand in my way. The commandant will be sorry," said Jozef.

In the meantime, Mother didn't go to sleep. She paced the floor and listened for any sound from the road. It was past twelve when she heard the horse's hooves. As the cart was approaching the house Bronica gathered her energy, jumped and ran home. Although it was dark, Mother was able to read from Bronica's face the horror she had suffered. Mother gathered her in her arms and held her for a long time.

CHAPTER THREE

1940

Rails grate, silence,
Unknown vastness, frozen camp,
Barbed wire, cry.

Our Christmas of 1939 was very sad. A dog and a cow were the only animals we had. Every morning before sunrise, our mother ran to the byre to milk the cow. She didn't have to wake up so early, but she wanted to make sure that the cow was still there.

It was Saturday, February 10, 1940. Our mother woke up very early. She was going to bake bread. She made leaven and was ready to milk the cow. When she opened the door, she saw two Russian soldiers and a sled. The soldiers pushed her back in and told her to wake everybody up. They searched the house for weapons. It frightened us and all the children started to cry. The dog barked as ferociously as he could.

"Get dressed and leave the house," the soldier ordered.

"We have no place to go. Who will take care of our property?" Mother protested.

"Show me everything that needs to be done, and I will take care of it."

While Mother wasted precious time leading the soldier to the barn, showing him grain for the chickens, and food for the cow, we dressed as best we could. "Don't forget to milk the cow," Mother added.

"Don't take too many things. You will be back soon," the soldier said.

Nevertheless, Bronica packed some food, clothing and bedding. She cried that one sled was not enough. Four of the youngest children and the things Bronica packed were all put on one sled. Mother, Bronica, Ema, and Michalina, had to walk all twenty-five kilometers, in very deep snow, to Pinsk, our nearest railroad station. Armed soldiers watched that nobody tried to escape. Soon, more and more sleds joined ours and we saw most of our neighbors. Children were crying from the cold, dogs were howling in the village, and cows mooed in the byre. The soldiers shot our dog, which had tried to follow us.

By late evening, we reached the station, and soldiers loaded us into freight cars, fifty people to a car. Some cars were full already. As soon as the car we were in was full, it was shut tight. The reality of the situation overwhelmed us. It became clear that we were going to Russia, and there was no chance that we would return soon. We felt like trapped animals.

Each car had four decks, two on each side. One small window provided the only light in the car. In the middle of the car stood an iron stove. Close to the door was a hole in the floor which served as a lavatory. What a monument to the culture of a victorious Russia!

During the night the train jerked violently as if it wanted to wake everybody up, and headed eastward. At the first stop more cars with people joined our transport. After four days we stopped at the Russian border. The border didn't truly exist anymore, but we had to change to Russian trains which rode on wider rail tracks.

As we marched from one train to another, there were many soldiers on horses. One horse grabbed Josephine's shoulder with his mouth and didn't let go. She cried and hung in mid-air. In all the confusion many children were crying. None of us noticed that she was missing. It was only after we took our place on the upper deck by the window that Mother started looking for Josephine. Panic stricken, she ran from car to car calling her name. Meanwhile, a soldier had pulled Josephine from the horse's mouth and started looking for her mother. After much screaming and calling, Mother found Josephine and brought her to our car.

Russian cars were also wider and each car had four windows. Soldiers ordered families with small children to take places by the windows. They probably wanted us to see as much as possible of their wretched country.

We used up our food. Other people were in the same situation. With so many people packed together lacking proper hygiene, lice were taking a heavy toll. Inside the car the walls glistened with frost. Sometimes the train stopped at a station and we got a pail of soup and some bread.

Our train changed direction from east to north. When someone asked the soldier where we were going, he said, "To the end of the tracks."

We seldom stopped at a station during the day, and never in a city. When we stopped at night, we were always at a little distance from a station. Two people from each car, with a pail and a sack, under the watchful eyes of soldiers, went to the station to get some bread and hot water. Sometimes they brought a pail of soup. This food was divided among everybody in the car. Sometimes we grabbed some snow to melt for water.

When we stopped at a station, soldiers went from car to car and ordered us to bring out the dead bodies. They were laid on the platform and we never knew what happened to them. Emotions are a luxury. Sadness and joy are expressed when there is hope for change. The people in the cars were hardened by the tragedy of war and their situation. Losing a member of the family was a very private matter. The expression of grief was not welcomed. Hungry and cold people welcomed death.

We traveled this way for a whole month. Thad's head was full of abscesses from cold. He was very sick. Helen fell off the deck onto a hot stove, and burned herself severely on her hands. Our mother took care of them the best she could. People were hungry, cold, sick, and above all had no will to live.

We had left Poland in February. At the end of April, we reached the end of the railroad tracks. The train stopped in an open field. The soldiers went from car to car and ordered everybody out. People fell into the deep snow. Many had difficulty getting up. The elderly tried to keep up, but cold, deep snow, and hunger sapped their energy. They fell frequently. Immediately, the victorious soldiers beat them with their guns. Many of them didn't get up at all. Mothers carried small children. Older children helped each other. Mother carried Thad on her back. Our neighbor Ed Adamski, only sixteen, carried Josephine on his back in the deep snow. The rest of us walked. We marched the whole night in the direction of lights flickering from a distant city.

Ed Adamski, his parents, and sister Eugenia were the most beautiful human beings we came across. In the car they had shared everything with us. Ed was very slim. He needed all the energy for himself, yet, without being asked, he offered his help.

In the morning, exhausted, frozen, and half dead, we reached the outskirts of Archangel. The soldiers directed us to a large theater from which all the seats had been removed. This theater had probably never seen such a human tragedy. People took every available spot. Everybody had to stand. It was impossible to go even to the lavatory for fear of being separated from one's family.

By noon, heaven be praised, we went to a restaurant for a sit-down dinner. It was difficult for us to believe in this show of humanity. People sobbed quietly, swallowing food mixed with tears. After dinner, many families were assigned to different labor camps and left the theater. It became possible to lie down on the floor.

Through the night, Thad cried and vomited. Our mother was unable to help him. In the morning she approached the person who had led us to the restaurant and asked for help. In a short time a nurse came and wanted to take Thad to the hospital. Although mother wanted him to go, she didn't want him to go alone. Thad was only five years old. A few nicely dressed Russian ladies wandered among the families and asked mothers to give up their children. They gave presents of warm clothing, shoes, sweets, and rolls. Mothers took the presents but held on to their children.

The nurse insisted that if Thad didn't go to the hospital he would die. He had a high fever. Our mother begged the nurse to let her go with Thad because he was too small and too sick to be alone in a strange place. The nurse must have had a good heart because she took our mother and Thad to the hospital. Bronica now had to take care of us.

We were in that theater for a whole week. One evening Bronica was called and told to get on a truck. She objected, saying that she couldn't leave her younger sisters, that she was responsible for us. Nothing helped. She was pushed on the truck, and they left. We had lost our mother, Thad, and now Bronica. The five of us sat on our few belongings and cried. The next morning two soldiers came, helped us with our things, and loaded us on a truck.

I don't remember how long we traveled. We slept and cried intermittently. The truck stopped and the soldiers told us to go into a large building. It looked like a factory. It was empty. We took our things with us. When we were inside, they locked the door behind us. It was dark and cold. We put our things on the floor and tried to lie down. We were sick from cold and exhaustion. Since they locked the door, we couldn't go to the bathroom. In the morning when the factory workers came, they had to clean up the floor. They screamed at us for this. They started a fire on the stove, boiled some water, and made some tea. One man wanted to give us some tea, but every time he came near us, we screamed. We thought that he wanted to beat us. We cried. They tried to talk to us, but we didn't understand them.

There was one old man among the workers who had false teeth. Out of desperation, he flipped them up. We gaped in amazement. None of us had ever seen dentures. We watched him with great curiosity. He flipped them in and out. We stopped crying and let him come close to us. He asked us what we were doing in their workshop. We understood only a few Russian and Belorussian words. Using those few words, and hands, we told him about our deportation, and we learned that we were in a labor camp in Siberia, near Archangel. The workers gave us some tea and bread. After this friendly encounter, they told us we couldn't stay there. They called the camp commandant. He came and told us to follow him. He gave us one small room in a barrack. This was also the room in which we found Bronica. We were very happy that we were together again.

Our room had only one steel bed without a mattress. In the next room was Natasha, Ignalo's wife, with only two of her children. The other children had died on the train and had been left on the platform. There was another neighbor of ours, a very old woman who by some accident was separated from her family. Her room was like a small, dark closet.

There were many buildings with many rooms. Each room contained a family. Each barrack had a long corridor with a single lavatory at one end and a small stove at the other. There was only one electric bulb on the ceiling in the corridor. This was the only light. The whole camp was surrounded by barbed wire. There were four watch towers with an armed guard in each, and a large gate. This gate was always open. There were funerals every day. The cemetery was near the gate, so traffic was never interrupted. Our camp address was:

> Archangelskaya Oblast
> Piervomajski Reyon
> Posiolok Uyma
> Kierepichny Zavod

The Russians in our labor camp were either deportees from Stalin's early purges, or released prisoners whose families' political ideology conflicted with Communism. Some of them were very friendly and told us about the circumstances that had brought them to Siberia. One guard, a young man about twenty, eagerly looked for company of Polish deportees and talked with them. His family in Russia had been wealthy. That was a crime, for which they were sent to Siberia. He was only a teenager when his parents died. Most of his life he spent in a labor camp and became a guard. His parents must have had a very positive influence on him and instilled in him the hate of Communism.

Once, he sang a song and later taught us the words. He also told us never, and he emphasized, never, sing it in public or even admit that we knew the words. This was more or less the theme and spirit of the song:

> *You are doomed, Mother Russia.*
> *I hope you will die soon. You bloodthirsty bastards.*
> *You call it ideological war,*
> *but all you do is steal, murder,*
> *and pack your pockets, while we soldiers*
> *rot in the trenches and die of starvation.*
> *Die soon, you, the most corrupted nation.*

When we sang this song at home, our mother almost fainted, and begged us never to sing it again. "It will be better if you forget it." She told us. These words will remain with me for the rest of my life.

CHAPTER FOUR

Labor Camp

Pale, sunken eyes,
Ravaged bodies, searching souls
If tomorrow comes?

From the first day, Bronica and Ema went to work in the brick factory mixing clay. They worked from six in the morning till six at night. Bronica was eighteen, and Ema was sixteen; Michalina was fourteen; Helena, twelve. I, Gryzelda, was nine, and Josephine, seven. The four of us stood in line for bread. Every time we came close to the store, older people pushed us away. By the time we entered the store, there was no bread. On our way back we got some hot water. When Bronica and Ema came home, tired and hungry, we added some salt to the hot water and that was our meal. We mixed it with our tears. Bronica tried to teach us how to stand in line. "Don't let anybody ahead of you once you have your place, or you will never buy anything." We listened and promised that tomorrow we wouldn't let anybody push us away.

That evening two Russian women came and said that

they needed help around the house. They would take Michalina and Helena with them the next morning. My sisters couldn't protest. They didn't know where they were going. That also meant that I would have to go alone for bread. I was so frightened by this responsibility that I couldn't sleep all night. Bronica and Ema, exhausted, huddled together on the floor in one corner. Michalina and Helena took the other side. Josephine and I took the rest of the space.

At night, I heard a soft knock at the door. Straining my ears, I heard somebody slide down the door. A weak voice called: "Bronica, Bronica, open the door and let me in. Please let me in. Some people came in and threw me out. I will give you all my property when we return to Poland."

She begged, promising more and more, but her voice was so weak, and Bronica was so tired that she didn't hear her. I strained my ears, but there was silence. I thought that she had gone away or fallen asleep. In the morning when Bronica opened the door, she found the woman frozen in a sitting position. Bronica informed the commandant on her way to work. The family of that unfortunate woman would never find out in what circumstances she died.

In the morning, when my sisters went to work, the Russian women came and took Michalina and Helena with them. They told me that Michalina would be in a nearby village, but Helena would go all the way to Archangel. It depended only on their goodwill whether my sisters would ever return.

I felt very lonely and lost. I didn't wake up Josephine. I decided it would be easier if I went for bread alone. It was a very cold morning; so I dressed as best I could and ran to stand in line. It was still very early, but the line was already very long. People bunched together for warmth. I joined them, and soon I found myself in the middle of a large mob.

At first, I was glad that there were so many people. It wasn't cold anymore, but people kept on pressing and I was getting short of breath. When the store opened, people pressed so hard that many fell, and the rest stepped over them. They trampled over me also. My nose was bleeding. I started to scream. I considered it a great disaster, because I lost my place in line, my face was bloodied, and there was little chance that I would get some bread. I must have screamed very hard because one sales lady came to me, wiped off my face, stopped the blood, and took me to the very beginning of the line. I bought two loaves of bread and went to our barrack. Later I took a pail and went to get some water. In the evening, when Bronica and Ema came from work, the four of us had some bread and water for dinner.

Every day I was getting more and more experienced in buying bread with the little money that our sisters earned. Sometimes, when there was an extra *ruble*, I went to a diner in the camp and bought a bowl of soup. Later, we diluted the soup with water to fill our stomachs.

In Siberia, the summer starts very late and is very short, but nature explodes with a profusion of fast growing flowers. Not far from the camp was a beautiful forest full of mushrooms and different kinds of berries. Despite the barbed wire, we could go out. Right behind the gate was a cemetery. Every day the number of graves increased. All the members of Ignalo's family died and were buried. Most of the families had someone dead, or whole families were completely wiped out.

Beyond the cemetery was a large forest. Arctic days were long, so after work we all went to the forest to find something to eat. This was a virgin forest with majestic trees which had been undisturbed by human presence. With the invasion of the shabbily dressed and hungry crowd, it would seem that the forest would be angered by our determination to disturb its serenity. Instead the forest was generous. It offered blueberries which were big and luscious. Filling our baskets, we ate as much as we could. On our return home we sorted out the leaves. In the morning on their way to work my sisters carried the baskets filled with berries and left me on the steps of a diner where I sold the berries. When people bought them, I felt very successful. Later, I went to buy bread and soup. Now we ate a little better. Our store, besides bread, carried some extra items, such as soap, herrings, and halvah. Sometimes it even had fabrics for dresses and blouses.

Our labor camp was far away from any town. The presence of small children, no adult males, and lack of food and money, killed any desire to escape. Archangel was the closest town, but it was separated from us by Dvina River. The only bridge over it was always guarded. Besides, where could we go? Identification documents were checked at every train station, and we had none.

One day I saw a group of people with sacks on their backs walking toward the camp. Among them was our mother. Not seeing Thad, I was convinced that he had died. Only later, I saw him tugging behind Mother. How did they know that we were in this camp? They didn't, but after leaving the hospital, they were told to go in this direction. They walked from Archangel, about twenty-five kilometers.

Thad had been in the hospital for eleven weeks. During that time Mother washed the floors and helped with the sick. Mother and Thad both looked good. The night they arrived, Mother prepared a meal with food she had saved from the hospital, and it was the first full meal we had since coming to the labor camp. This was also the first night that Bronica could really rest.

The next day, our mother went to work in the brick

factory. She had to load two hundred raw bricks onto a cart and push the cart on rails to a shed. There, she had to unload the bricks onto shelves to let them dry. It was easier during the summer, but in winter the bricks froze and were slippery. When there was ice on the rail, the cart often slipped, scattering the bricks. Our mother could never make her quota of one thousand bricks per day.

Bronica was transferred to the sheds. She loaded the dried bricks on carts and took them to the ovens to be fired. She liked this work better because very often a few cows would take shelter in the shed, and she could milk them. Bronica did that in great secrecy, and sometimes she brought some milk home. If she had been caught, she would have been sent to a much harder labor camp away from us.

During harvest time people from the brick factory went to work digging potatoes and carrots, and cutting cabbages. Those cabbage heads were so large that often it took two girls to lift one. Cabbage leaves were thick and juicy. People would secretly break a leaf to eat. After a day's work they received some potatoes, carrots and maybe the smallest cabbage head that could be found.

Hunger forced us to do things that in normal times we would have been ashamed to even consider. During the night, workers went to the fields and stole cabbages, potatoes, and carrots. Somehow, the head of the *kolhoz* (collective farm) found out that people were stealing and started guarding the fields. Russians were stealing also. They said that it was not stealing because "in Russia everything that is yours is mine." We liked their explanation and stole enough cabbage to make a small barrel of sauerkraut.

Once, during the day, I went to the field and pulled a cabbage. On my way home I saw a guard on a horse with a gun. I was terribly frightened and looked for a place to hide. There was not a blade of grass to hide me. I squatted down to be as small as possible and hoped the guard wouldn't notice me. He galloped toward me. I was petrified. When he was near, he suddenly turned his horse and galloped back as if he had forgotten something. I stood and ran as fast as I could, leaving the cabbage behind. In the evening I went back and retrieved my treasure.

Thad was not so lucky. He went out in the field one day where workers were picking the cabbages. He sat by one and started breaking off leaves and eating them. The guard came and started beating him. He hit him over and over again. Thad was bloodied all over. He cried, but the beating continued. He lost the energy to cry and just stood there, open to all the savage blows. Josephine saw what was happening and started screaming. The guard would have killed Thad if women workers had not interfered and promised that Thad would never do it again. The woman brought him to the barrack all bruised and bloody. From this moment, Thad seldom left the barrack and slept most of the time. Josephine stayed with him. Thad and Josephine were only awakened when there was something to eat. There was not a single toy to entertain them, nor a scrap of paper or pencil to stimulate their minds.

In August our commandant called the children to find out which ones could go to school. Since my Russian was very limited I was placed in the first grade. We were promised that later it would be decided whether Josephine and Thad would go to school. In Poland I would have finished the third grade, but in Siberia I was in the first grade. I had always liked school and was happy now that I was chosen. My new status carried certain privileges. I received new shoes, a Consomol's (Communist youth organization) uniform, and a red bandanna. I had to wear the uniform every day to school.

My first days in school were very difficult. With my limited Russian I was lost, and children were making fun of me. By December, I was as good as any other child, and could read better than many of them. We didn't celebrate Christmas at school, but for the New Year we had a party. "Grandfather Frost" came and gave every child some sweets.

Those were our first holidays in exile. Michalina and Helena had not returned. We hadn't heard from them since they had left. The only bright spot in this holiday was Bronica's marriage. There were many young people Bronica's age in our labor camp, and romance can bloom under the most difficult circumstances. Sometimes after work, the people gathered together for a song and friendly chat. One young man, Bruno, paid special attention to Bronica. Although she liked him, she didn't want to encourage him and build up his hopes. She still remembered her boyfriend she had left in Poland.

Yet, it happened. Bronica become convinced that she might have a future with Bruno. On New Year's Eve in 1940 Bronica, with Bruno, went to the commandant's office and signed their names. The commandant called them husband and wife, and that was the end of the ceremony. On their return to the barrack, we had bread with herring and onion. We also had a bottle of vodka, but with so little food, everybody was drunk after one shot. Our mother was happy for Bronica. Bruno was a very good mechanic, and our family needed a man to take care of us.

The winter was very hard. We survived on dried mushrooms and berries, and on the stolen cabbage from which we made sauerkraut.

One day the commandant of the camp came to the

factory where my mother worked and told her to come to his office after work. Mother was petrified and expected the worst. After work, on rubbery legs, and with her heart in her throat, she knocked at the office door. She entered, and on the table she saw a parcel which was opened. Scattered on the table around the box were a package of sugar, bars of soap, a slab of bacon, a sack of flour, spools of thread, and needles.

"This package was sent to you. Who is Sabina?"

Mother couldn't believe her eyes, and didn't quite understand what he was saying.

"Who is Sabina?" the commandant asked again, a little louder.

"Sabina is Bronica's friend from Lahishyn. They went to the seventh grade together."

"Your daughter has a very good friend. Take this package. It is yours."

My mother packed everything inside the box and carried her treasure to the barrack. We enjoyed good meals for several days. We were all uplifted by the generosity of a friend. Sabina, who had finished only the seventh grade, had been able to find us and send us the things we needed most, while my mother's educated family, although they knew that we were deported, never got in contact with us. Two months later, Sabina sent us another package. Bronica wrote to her several times but never received an answer.

In January the commandant of our camp called my mother and told her that Josephine and Thad would go to school.

"I am very happy that the three of them will go to school together," she replied.

"No, Josephine and Thad will go away to school. They will have good food and clothing, and there will be experienced people to take care of them. They will be raised to be good citizens."

"They will go only if Gryzelda goes with them to take care of them," our mother objected. But I didn't know what my mother expected of me if I went with Josephine and Thad.

The commandant didn't want to take me and said that I was too old for that school. He yelled, "Your children will go whether you like it or not. If you won't let them go, you will be sorry."

Two weeks later, he repeated his ultimatum.

"No," Mother said.

The next day in school, my teacher told me that I could no longer attend the school and I should return my uniform and shoes. That ended my education. Josephine and Thad remained home.

After Bronica was married, the whole family moved from the one little room to a one-room hut. The wooden floor, with cracks between the boards, lay directly on the dirt. It was cool during the summer, but in the winter water froze in the pail and the walls glistened with frost.

Though the hut was more spacious, it was a terrible burden on me. Previously I could get the water for cooking and washing only a few steps away. Now I had to walk at least half a kilometer, rain or shine, summer or winter. The only water we had was what I brought in a pail.

During winter, I had to lower the pail into a deep hole. By the time I brought it up, half was spilled and half was frozen. I was not able to make more than two trips, so washing and laundry had to be forgotten.

In the back of the hut was a potato field with an armed guard. One day, when all the potatoes were dug, I took Thad and Josephine into the field. We pretended that we were playing, but we were looking for potatoes that had been left. I found two and put them into my pocket. When we looked for more, the guard came and told us to empty our pockets. He screamed at us and threatened to put us in prison if he saw us again. He called us thieves who robbed Mother Russia.

There was not much sickness, but people often died of starvation. Families tried to conceal the deaths so they could continue to receive the full bread ration. When this "crime" was discovered, the whole family was punished and lost their bread rations for a few days.

One day, a Russian woman from Archangel came to our barrack and told my mother, "I need some help. I think that Gryzelda can take care of my baby."

My mother was reluctant to let me go, because there would be no one to get bread and to take care of Josephine and Thad. This lady was a teacher. She lived with her two-month-old baby and her mother, in a two-bedroom apartment with a small kitchen and a bathroom. That was a luxury. I wanted to go because Helena was in Archangel, and I thought that I might see her.

I left with the lady. When we got to her apartment, I immediately went to the baby, but the grandmother ordered me, "Stay away from the baby. You will wash the baby's diapers, wash the dishes, and sweep the floor." Those were the only things they allowed me to do. Also, I was to stay in the baby's room and nowhere else. During the night, I slept under the baby's crib. The only food they gave me was a small and very fat fish that looked like a sardine. The fish were kept in a pail of water, until fished out and given to me. The fish were not only very fat but also very salty. I didn't get a crumb of bread with it.

After one week on such a diet I became violently sick and was always on the run to the bathroom. In the second week

I could hardly get up. That is when the teacher and her mother decided that they would soon send me back home. They claimed that I was too much trouble. I made too much dust while sweeping the floor, the diapers were not very clean. I suspected that I had been sent there to be punished for the school incident with the commandant.

One morning, when I felt a little better, the teacher's mother told me, "Get dressed. There is a group of people going towards Uyma, you will go with them." Uyma was the nearest village to our labor camp. I was terribly weak and couldn't keep up with the group. I rested, and often I had to run to catch up with the others. We had left Archangel in the morning, and now it was getting dark. I didn't know how much farther I had to go.

Finally we reached Uyma; the last woman in the group left, and I was alone. The woman had told me to go directly toward the lights in front of me. I was afraid of wolves and of drowning in the snow, but I had no choice, so I forged forward. In the darkness I noticed a long column of tanks. I dug a hole in the snow and hid myself. When the soldiers passed by me, and I could no longer hear them, I resumed my walk. Late in the night, with my last spark of energy, I reached our barrack. My mother was surprised when I told her why I came. We both cried.

The deportees had finished all the food stored for the winter, and now all they had was 400 grams of bread for each working adult and 200 grams for a child. The traffic to the cemetery increased.

Was this winter ever going to end? I looked through the window at the vastness of the fields covered with snow. Days were getting a little longer. It meant that we felt hunger a little longer. We felt lost and forgotten. Even spring forgot us and was taking its time. The sun occasionally sent a warmer ray our way. I didn't give up and kept looking out the window for a change of weather. The drab emptiness inside and out of the window was devastating. Only hope of spring kept me glued to the window.

One day, I spotted a little puddle formed by melting snow, promising that spring was on its way. It was coming slowly, bashfully, measuring its progress, but it definitely was on its way.

The day was filled with promise. I went out and walked on the road, looking for other signs of spring. While I was busy looking, I fell into a ditch full of melting snow. The ditch was quite deep and the water reached to my arms. I tried to get out, but couldn't find any solid ground. After what seemed like hours, I escaped out of it, all wet and frozen. In the barrack I warmed and dried myself by the stove. Now everywhere I went, I had to be very careful until all the snow had melted. Spring had arrived, and its messengers, snowdrops, lifted their heads above the snow.

On a warm, beautiful day when the sun was brightly shining, I came home with our bread in the afternoon, boiled some water, and tried to wake up Josephine and Thad to give them something to eat. Josephine woke up quickly, but I had trouble waking up Thad. I called him, shook him, but he didn't react. I ran to the next barrack to ask for help. One woman came and she started shaking him. Thad looked dead. I left the woman and ran out to call my mother and tell her that Thad was dead.

The factory buildings were far away and I didn't know where my mother worked. I ran, and not paying attention to the road, I fell a few times. By the time I reached the factory, I was exhausted. I looked into every building and called: "Mother, Mother, Mother!" In the last one I found my mother and started screaming: "Mother, come home! Thad is dead!"

Mother ran to her supervisor. "I beg you, let me go home. My son is dead."

"Go back to work."

"Please let my mother go. My brother is dead," I cried.

"Go back and finish your work."

We both cried and begged. The supervisor insisted that Mother should finish her work. After a while he let her go. By the time we reached the exit from the factory, the whistle blew announcing the end of the work day. We ran like demented souls.

The old woman who had stayed with Thad had given him a massage and a hot compress. When he opened his eyes, she gave him some sweet water. By the time we reached the barrack, Thad was sitting up looking around with glazed eyes. Mother took over and gave him some bread. He ate all of our bread, so Mother and I drank some warm water. Later we all went to sleep.

Once, I saw Michalina in the store. She said that she was fine, she was treated well and didn't suffer hunger.

We received news from Archangel that Helena was in the hospital with pneumonia. One Sunday, Bronica went to the hospital to visit her. Bronica recounted to us: "It was a large, two-story building. I was surprised to see so much activity and hear so many screams. I found out in the office that Helena was on the second floor. To get to the stairs leading to the second floor, I passed the length of the first floor. I saw wards filled with wounded soldiers. I was frightened and rushed upstairs. Looking through the second floor ward, I found Helena. She seemed to be so small on her bed, and lost under the covers. `How are you Helena? How did you get here?'

"'I was sick with a cold for over a month, she told me. The woman I worked for didn't do anything about it, but when I developed a high fever, she was afraid that her baby would catch my illness. She sent me to the hospital.' This conversation seemed to exhaust her.

"The head nurse called me to the office. 'You can come back to see your sister in two weeks. She is doing better, but she is still very weak. We need help in the hospital. Would you like to work as a nurse's aide?'

"'I don't think I could work with sick and dying people,' I said. The head nurse dismissed me. I went to Helena again and told her that I would come back in two weeks."

Bronica had seen too many dead bodies in her short life. She knew hospital work would be overwhelming.

In two weeks Bronica went back to the hospital. Helena was on the road to recovery. At the same time, Helena's employer was there making plans to take Helena home with her.

In the summer of 1941 we heard the news that Germany had declared war on Russia. We accepted it as a good sign and hoped that those murderous nations would wipe each other out. We started dreaming about our freedom. Then the news came. AMNESTY!

We were paralyzed with disbelief. Our most secret dreams had come true. We were free. Now we were allies of Russia fighting Germany. The Polish Army was organized in southern Russia, and all men were asked to join it. Amnesty also affected civilians. They could leave the labor camps and follow the army. People felt full of life, and started planning their future. Most of the men left their work, took some food, and started on the long journey to freedom. Some took their families with them, or promised to send for them when they reached the army.

Many families, ours included, could only dream. We had no money for train tickets. We had no money for bread. In our family four people were working. But we never had enough money to last us from one payday to the next. As a matter of fact, when payday came my mother didn't get paid because she always owed them money for the bread we received in the store on credit.

One day after getting our portions of bread I had a little time, so my friends and I decided to pick some sorrel. There was a beautiful meadow not too far away. To reach it, we had to cross Dvina River. There was no bridge but floating logs. Having more courage than brains, slowly, from log to log, we crossed the river. The sorrel was plentiful and beautiful, with large and succulent leaves. We ate some, enjoying the refreshing sourness.

We heard noise in the distance. A band of Russian Consomols ran our way, calling us nasty names. They also screamed that they would drown us. We didn't wait for them to repeat their threats. We ran toward the river and jumped onto the logs. The boys chased us, screaming constantly. We managed to jump from log to log. Many circuses would have been proud of our acrobatics. We safely reached the other shore, only a little wet, but without sorrel.

By now we had sold everything we had and the only thing left was my mother's wedding band, but it was broken. She went to the village, entered every house trying to sell her wedding band for some food. Nobody wanted to buy it, but one decent soul swapped a small sack of potatoes for it. Our mother came home with her bounty. She washed and boiled the potatoes without peeling them, so as not to waste anything.

Malnutrition not only sapped our energies, but I was beginning to have nightmares. One night I dreamed that mother waited for all of us to fall asleep so she could slash our throats. The next night before we went to sleep, I made sure that all the knives were hidden. The nightmare had been so horrible that I kept watch all night long. Mother couldn't turn from side to side without scaring me. I also got up and checked on everybody, making sure they were alive. By morning I was exhausted. There was nothing to eat when mother came from work that day. I had another sleepless night. In the morning some women were going berry picking. My mother asked me to go with them.

Exhausted and hungry I could hardly keep up with the women, I had to rest often and then run and look for someone. I was afraid I would be lost. I didn't pick any berries and came home with an empty basket. Mother was terribly disappointed, but Bronica managed to buy some bread, so each one of us had a slice and a cup of hot water.

The next day was Saturday, so after work my mother, Bronica, Ema, and I went berry picking. This time we filled four large baskets. We came home happy. On Sunday morning, very early, Bronica, Ema, and I went to Archangel with our berries. It was a long and hard journey. First we had to walk about four kilometers, then take a tram, change, and take another one. By eleven o'clock we were in Archangel.

We took the corner of one busy street. We were very successful. People were buying quickly. In a short time we sold all our berries. Happy, we started our way home. We stopped to buy some bread. As the matter of fact, we loaded our baskets with loaves of bread. We also treated ourselves to soup and took some home. What a feast it was when we arrived! We were not hungry anymore and that evening I didn't hide the knives, and slept soundly.

One day another woman came to our barrack and said that she wanted me to go with her to take care of her baby. The woman was in the military service and her post was not very far away. She checked on the baby every weekend.

During the week I would be alone with the baby. Having had a bad previous experience, I was afraid of the responsibility. The woman promised twenty rubles a month (one kilogram of bread cost one ruble and five kopecks). She also promised that I would have a bed to sleep in, and that she would share her food with me. I went with her. It was a welcome change. As I took care of the baby, and gave Mother my money, my nightmares faded away. The baby was only three months old. I was astonished that the mother entrusted such a young baby to me. I don't know how I managed, but she was pleased with my help.

At the end of each month when my mother came to get the money, she always heard how well I did. I was glad that my mother came so that I didn't have to take the money home. I was afraid of going through the cemetery where often I had to run away from wolves. I stayed at this job for only three months because the camp commandant ordered everybody to get back to the camp. The mother of the baby was sorry to see me go. The day I left, she watched me get dressed. I tied my shoes with ropes and put some straw inside them to keep my feet warm. When she saw that, she felt pity and offered me her "valonki," beautiful high boots woven from pure wool.

"Try them on, Gryzelda."

I put them on and they reached all the way to my hips.

"I want you to wear them while you are going home, but let your mother return them because I need them."

"I am grateful for your compassion and trust, and I can assure you that you will get them back."

The next day after work, my mother took the valonki back to the owner, and again thanked her for her kindness.

The war must have been very bad for Russia. Now, after work in the brick factory, everybody had to go into the fields to dig potatoes, carrots, and other vegetables. The army needed food and there were not enough workers. With all those vegetables, the guards tried to prevent anybody from taking even a bite of a carrot.

Bronica worked very hard in the hope of getting some flour and vegetables to bring home. That day, by noon time she had no energy left and fainted. The rest of the day she lay in a furrow gathering enough strength to get home. At the end of the day, she received a cup of flour.

Working every day, constantly hungry, Bronica reached her desperation point. She decided not to go to work until she was paid what was owed her, so we could buy some bread. She had support from most of the workers because everybody was in the same situation. The commandant called her a trouble-maker and organizer. For this sign of courage, Bronica was sent to prison in Archangel for three months. Mother and Bruno, Bronica's husband, were desperate. Our friendly guard found out which prison Bronica was in, and tried to assure our mother that at least she would get some food.

Most of the food harvested was sent to the army. The rest, like potatoes, cabbage, carrots, and sunflowers, were saved for the animals. Workers didn't fit into this scheme, but they found a way to survive. They dug deep holes, lined them with straw, and filled them with potatoes. They did the same with carrots. To the holes with cabbage and sunflowers they added salt, and covered the holes with straw and dirt. When they finished this work, it was difficult to see where the vegetables were hidden, but those who worked with them remembered very well. During the night they went back and dug out the potatoes, cabbages, and carrots. This was how they stayed alive and saved their families.

One day, we found out that the brick factory would be

closed, and everybody would go to work on a *sovhoz* (a state farm). The *sovhoz* we were going to was in southern Russia, near Tashkent. We didn't know where Tashkent was, but the idea of leaving this frozen, lice- and bedbug-ridden place lifted our spirits. People in the camp were farmers and had dreamed of getting back on farms. The commandant of our camp took care to secure the necessary papers and tickets for everybody. Since my mother still owed them money, our tickets had to be on credit. We were to pay it back after we started working.

Health workers came from headquarters to help with the liquidation of the camp. First they ordered us to take baths. There was a public bath, but it had never been opened. Now, they decided to take advantage of this commodity, and went from barrack to barrack, counting everybody, and assigning them a special hour when they were to take baths. There was no discrimination. Twenty people took baths simultaneously, regardless of age or sex. First, you had to strip and leave your clothes on hangers. No spring-cleaning was done more thoroughly. The clothes were steamed, scorched, and dried. This killed lice, but the hot steam shrank the wool and people had to squeeze into their clothes afterwards. After disrobing you were ready to take a bath in an enormous room filled with steam. The heat took your breath away, and you were completely disoriented. This lasted about ten minutes, and when you thought you just couldn't take it any longer, you were drenched with cold water. After this rinse, we formed a line, received a small cake of soap, and started washing ourselves. We were supervised all the time, and made aware of the great benefits awarded through the generosity and great understanding of Father Stalin. "Take advantage of his great heart, and try to look like people, not pigs. You all smell like pigs! Why don't you bathe more often?"

Bruno supplied us with potatoes and other food, but it

was a very dangerous task. If caught, he would have lost the amnesty privileges and would have been sent to prison. Our mother agreed to go to the *sovhoz*, but she didn't want to leave Bronica behind. Bruno also wanted to wait for her release, because he wanted to join the Polish Army.

The first group of people was ready within two weeks. These were older men and adolescent boys, who were to prepare the living quarters for the coming families. Women and children were to follow later. "Later" extended to two months. People spent not only the money they had, but also borrowed heavily against their future wages. Our mother was the heaviest borrower, but after all, there would be four working people in the family when we reached Tashkent, so everything would be paid back.

CHAPTER FIVE

Departure

Distant yesterday,

Frightening tomorrow,

Moon-less night, daybreak.

After spending two years in Uyma, the word that we would leave finally came on December 19, 1941. Tashkent would be the land of our future, with December 19 the first day of our new life. Life would be better. Growing things always signify a better life.

Our transport was to leave on January 6, 1942. Mother kept everything ready, but said she wouldn't move until Bronica's return. It was already January 3. Mother and Bruno were worried sick. In the evening, while we were sipping potato soup, the door suddenly opened and Bronica stood there with a sack on her back. We didn't recognize her at first, but soon, through tears, we hugged her and bombarded her with questions. She looked good. She was clean and was wearing nice clothes. We were all very much surprised at her wealth until she told us how she got it.

She started with her arrest: "When they brought me to prison, there was another person my age who was sentenced for six months. They locked us up together. We cried the rest of the day and the entire night. The next day, we volunteered for work, and washed the floors. Later, they told us that since we volunteered, we could move to a larger cell with two beds with sheets. We had three meals a day. We worked hard all day long, and nobody bothered us during the night. Many of the women had been charged with different crimes like murder, robbery, and assault. We were afraid of them, but they didn't do us any harm."

Bronica continued: "My roommate was born in Russia of Polish parents who were deported after the 1863 Uprising. Her room at home in Archangel had a torn curtain and the light was visible outside. This was the time of blackout. She was accused of being a spy and giving light signals.

"After three months in prison I was free to go, and they let me out. Not knowing where to go, or what to do, I stood by the gate, looked around, felt terribly lost, and started to cry. The guard looked at me for a long time. He approached me screaming, and I was scared that he would take me back. He came closer and said, 'Go to the Polish Consulate in Archangel.' He gave me directions and explained how to get there.

"'Take these ten rubles,' he said smiling, and handed them to me.

"I thanked him and went looking for the consulate. I found the place. The consul was very much interested in my story. He was the nicest human being I have ever met in my life. He instructed his secretary to take me to the bathroom so I could take a bath. While I was scrubbing myself the secretary brought in all new clothes. Cleaned and dressed, I sat at the table for an afternoon meal. The consul asked me many questions, and the secretary made some notes. At the end of our conversation he gave me one hundred rubles and urged me to get back to our camp as soon as I could because everybody was leaving Uyma, for the *sovhoz* in southern Russia. Uplifted in spirit, and with a full stomach, I took the tram to Uyma."

The next day Bruno left to join the army. The rest of us anxiously waited for our departure.

When we had been deported to Siberia in February 1940, many other villagers who were Belorussians and Ukrainians were deported with us. When we were originally registered in the labor camp and asked our place of birth, those people had claimed they were born in Russia. Now when we were leaving Uyma, they wanted to leave also, but the authorities told them that they, as Russian citizens, had to stay in their own country. Justice was done. They stayed in Siberia and were not allowed to leave the camp.

Early on January 6, the trucks took us to the railroad station in Archangel. We were registered again, but the officials said Bronica couldn't get on the train. She didn't have her papers. Desperate, she went back to the consul, who went with her to the prison. There the consul demanded Bronica's papers. The prison commandant claimed that he didn't have any papers and asked them to leave. The consul, exerting his authority, demanded Bronica's papers. He also demanded that the commandant himself should look for them. After long negotiations and threats, the commandant agreed to give Bronica the release papers. They grabbed the papers, and in the consul's car sped to the station. Bronica jumped into our railroad car at the last moment, just as the train started moving. The consul waved, and wished us a safe journey to a free Poland. His wish reverberated in our ears, but Poland was so far away, and right then our destination was a *sovhoz* in southern Russia.

There were seven cars with 342 people, the last survivors from Uyma. People were frightened. Some wondered aloud if going so far was a good idea. Would we ever get there, and with the war going on, wouldn't it be better to stay in one place? The train was merciless and moved away from the station. People talked of their suffering, of all those who had not survived, and of the brutalities toward the dispossessed.

As we reached Vologda, our train was pushed to the side track to make room for a military transport. We were not sure how long the train would stay. People were penned in their cars. During the night there was a shuffling and reshuffling of trains. With a sharp jerk we were on our way again. After a few longer stops we reached Moscow. Here again we witnessed trains of soldiers heading west. We were far away from the city, couldn't buy anything, and had eaten all our food. People were hungry. During the stop at Moscow, they walked around the station and trains scavenging for food and begging.

I left our car in hope of finding something to eat. Walking along the platform, looking at the buildings overhanging the station, I smelled pancakes. If I could only get to that kitchen, I thought desperately, maybe I could get something to eat. I lowered myself on the rails, slipped under the cars, and found stairs leading up to a room from which the smell was coming. Slowly I climbed the stairs and gently knocked at the door. A young woman opened the door and was very surprised to see me. Through the open door I saw a very small kitchen and a baby sitting in a high chair. On the stove was a pan with pancakes. I told the woman that I was very hungry, and that I had come to her door because I smelled her pancakes. I hoped that she would give me some. She gave me four, and put the next batch on to fry. Meanwhile, she asked me hundreds of questions. She wanted to know where I came from, where I was going, how many people were in the train, what we were doing in Russia, and so on. I ate as fast as I could, burning my mouth, and answering the questions as best I could. I was also very anxious to go, fearful that our train would leave without me. She gave me another batch and asked me to stay so she could make some more. As hungry as I was, I thanked her and ran as fast as I could to find our car. Before I reached the car, I ate all the pancakes. I felt guilty that I didn't bring any for the rest of the family. Hunger makes us behave like animals.

The train stayed in Moscow for three days. During the following night we moved again. After a short while the train stopped and there was a deafening silence. In the morning people looked through the window and saw snow reaching the doors and emptiness as far as one could see. Our seven cars were destined for extinction. All that was necessary for our deaths was that we be left here for two weeks. We burned the boards from the decks of the cars to keep warm, and melted snow for water, which we drank mixed with our tears.

Five of the strongest boys took the initiative to go to Moscow to notify the authorities and ask for help. They decided to go south along the railroad tracks.

As we waited for their return, time went by very slowly. We kept the stove burning only during the night. The upper decks were reduced to a few boards and everybody squeezed on to the lower decks. Depression gnawed at people's minds. The silence was often interrupted by children's coughing and the quiet sobbing of adults.

There was fear for the boys. Maybe they were all frozen, maybe they went the wrong way and never reached Moscow, and maybe they were not coming back? Since there was no food, there was fear that we would soon start dying. Every few hours families and friends would call each other's names to see if they were still alive. If somebody took his time answering, there were sobs and hysterics. People started

seeing things, and their ears strained for the sound of a locomotive. Maybe the Germans were in Moscow, and the boys
were captured? We would all die.

Five days passed. During that time not even one train
passed by, although there were other tracks nearby. On the
sixth day we heard the sound of a train. Who was it?
Germans or our help? If these were Germans and they knew
that we were in the cars, they would kill us all. Just the
thought of it drove people to desperation. The train just
passed us by. A few hours later another train approached,
stopped across from us, and went back. Then everybody was
convinced that they were Germans. Nobody uttered a sound.
People were afraid that the beating of their own hearts would
give them away.

Josephine suddenly screamed from hunger spasms, and
Mother gave her some sweet water. She drank and became
blue from pain. One woman dug deep into her sack and
produced a piece of dry bread. Our mother soaked it in the
water; Josephine ate it and became quiet.

The train started back toward us and was getting closer
and closer. Then there was a sharp bump. It attached itself to
our cars and we were on the way. Then a new fear paralyzed
everybody: Germany had won the war. They were taking us
to Germany. People lost their will and energy, and since they
couldn't do anything about it, they resigned themselves to
their fates.

After a long while we reached Moscow again. The train
stopped and the five boys jumped out of the locomotive. They
went from car to car with sacks of bread. Many prayed, cried,
and hugged each other, grateful for a saved life. Some women
went to buy soup. Our five heroes went from car to car and
told everybody how they got help.

"We went south because it seemed the most logical

direction. We followed along the railroad tracks, and very often we had to dig out the snow to see the tracks. By the second night we were terribly tired, so when we reached a small station, we had to stop. Everything was burned down except a small, half-burned hut. We stopped there for the night. Another thing that drew us to that hut was the smell of burned meat. When we reached the hut, my friends went after that meat, and in the darkness of the night took chunks of it and ate. I was the last one to get in and collapsed from exhaustion. In the morning they saw that the meat could have been from either a human or a dog. Both of them were equally burned. We shot out from that place, and while walking my friends debated which was worse, human or dog meat.

"In Moscow we went to the transportation authorities with the information that seven cars of people, who were going to a *sovhoz* to produce food for the Russian Army, were stranded, and hungry. We waited a few hours for their answer. Late into the night they told us to go to the station, get the bread, and get on the locomotive which would take us back to our train."

People wanted to hear this story over and over again, and the boys gladly repeated it.

We were on our way again, but surprisingly we were going north instead of south toward Tashkent. The train didn't stop for the entire day, then after shuffling and re-shuffling, we were connected to a transport of coal and headed back. Moscow, here we come for the third time. What a wretched city! Why can't we get away from you? This time after a very short stop, the train left. We reached Kalinin, and the train stopped. The soldiers surrounded our train and ordered everybody out. Some people couldn't straighten out their legs after having been sitting in squatting positions for such a long time. The soldiers looked for men of military age. The boys they found were too young. After a close inspection, we were allowed to get back into our cars.

The train moved again, but to everybody's surprise, we were going west. We passed small towns, villages, open fields. We stopped at one station to give way to a military train. Another train, this time a cargo train with open platforms filled with salt, stopped opposite us. People ran to the platforms and filled their sacks with salt. Ema jumped out barefoot from our car and brought in two large lumps of salt. For the next few days we added salt to our water.

Our directions changed a few more times. When we reached the next station we found out that there was a lack of salt. It was possible to trade it for other food. We sold our salt by kilograms. There was no way to weigh it, and besides, people mixed salt with snow to make it heavier. We bought two loaves of bread, pancakes, some cereal, and a liter of milk. What a luxury! It was the first time since we had left Uyma that we had enough to eat. At the next stop nobody wanted salt. They needed sugar and matches. We had not come across those items yet. The direction of our train was erratic. People tried to analyze the confusion and to plot the progress of the war.

We reached a station. Our train pulled next to a train full of flour. People jumped out from their cars and tried to take some of it. A policeman appeared and tried to scare us away with his gun. He also chased Bronica. White flour covered her navy blue coat. She ran to our car, jumped on the upper deck and grabbed a baby. She pinched the baby, which gave a loud scream. The policeman got into the car and tried to pull her from the upper deck, to take her to the police station. Women started screaming that the reason they were stealing the flour was that they were dying of starvation. They asked the policeman to get out. Waving his pistol, he cursed them and threatened to shoot Bronica. Some women were frightened and asked Bronica to go, others told her to stay. The baby screamed. Having experienced prison before, Bronica refused to leave the car. Providence came to our aid, because the train started to move and was gathering speed. The policeman had no choice. Jumping out of the car, he threatened to shoot us all. The train left the station. We lived, but we didn't get any flour. Why did the policeman let Bronica enter the car? He could have taken her directly to the police station.

We never knew in which direction the train would go, or how long it would stay at a station. We were afraid to go far in search of food. If the train left us, we could find ourselves back in the labor camp. Once, Michalina had the misfortune to be left behind. Later, she told us how it happened.

"Very early in the morning, when the train stopped at the station, a small group from each car went to look for food. Bronica went with the group that was looking for the bread. The bakery was nearby, so they bought the bread and returned to their train, which was already moving. Bronica was the last one to jump onto the steps between the cars.

"I was with the group that looked for soup. We had to go far. When we found the diner it was still closed, so we went back, but our train was gone. We didn't know where the train went, but at the station we explained that we were going to the *sovhoz* in Tashkent, and that there were seven cars of people. They asked us to wait. There weren't that many trains going in the same direction. We waited at the station the whole day. Late in the evening we were ushered into a passenger train, but still without food. It took us three days to reach Arys, a very large railroad station. There, they told us that we might find our train. We went from train to train knocking at every car. After a long time we found our train.

Everybody greeted us as if we were ghosts. My mother had lost all hopes of ever seeing me again.

"The next time I got off the train I had better luck, but I almost froze to death. The train stopped to get some fuel and water. Nearby was an open market, so I went to get some pancakes. I took some salt with me to trade for food, bought pancakes, and then noticed that our train was moving. I ran as fast as I could, and, with the last drop of energy, I grabbed the handle of the open platform, and pulled myself on. A blast of cold air and snow almost knocked me off the platform. I sat, held on to the side, and must have fallen asleep. The strong jerk of the stopping train awakened me. I wanted to get up but I couldn't move. Then I realized that if I didn't get up and find our car, I would freeze to death. With all the determination I could muster, I slid from the platform and, as stiff as a rod, I went to our car. The pancakes were frozen in my hands. I had to be pulled into the car."

As we traveled, we tried to go back in our memory and figure out where we were, and if we would ever get to our destination. We remembered passing Vologda, our first major stop, and passing that wretched Moscow three times. We had passed Zyran, Kuybyshev, Chkalov, and Orsk. Our train went south through Aralsk, from Kazakhstan into Uzbekistan. We had left Archangel on January 6. It was now the end of February, and we were not even close to our destination. Many doubted that we would ever reach Tashkent. This thought made them despondent and depressed.

Hunger was ever present. We became like the locust. The minute the train stopped, everybody ran out in search for food. At one station there was an open car with a dead horse in it. People jumped on it like vultures and tore it to pieces not wondering about the cause of the horse's death. They boiled the meat on their little stoves and ate it. Our mother couldn't overcome her aversion to the horse's meat and, hungry, quietly sobbed in the corner. We told her that we ate everything. At the next stop Bronica took her last pair of woolen socks and traded them for a cup of cereal. Later, she cooked the cereal with some meat and gave it to mother, claiming that it was not the horse's meat.

The scenery and the climate changed constantly. From Kazan to Kuybyshev we passed through the Kazakhs' country with steppes and prairies. We never stopped at stations, but in the steppes, or open fields. Kazakhs come to the train with milk, pancakes, eggs, and bread to trade for other goods. The only thing we could trade was whatever was included in the transport. We had too much salt. We took whatever the Kazakhs had to offer, and asked them to help themselves to our things. Sometimes the train left before they had time to take anything, and screams and curses followed. We couldn't help it. The instinct for survival was strong. We felt ashamed, but hunger dulled our conscience.

The train went through the steppes of Kazakhstan. What a terrible emptiness! Sometimes on the horizon we could see clay-built cottages. The climate was getting warmer. When we passed through the steppe, the grass was tall. It looked more like October instead of March. We had to get there before the planting season, otherwise, we would starve to death over the winter.

There were some passengers whose spirits thrived on adversity. They were found in every car. In our car, one very old woman never complained. The harder it became, the more she was convinced that with the help of God we would overcome our misery and our future would be better. She had suffered much in her life. The suffering made her stronger. Every morning and evening she sang religious songs and encouraged everybody to join in singing. At first, reluctantly, a few

voices joined hers, but soon they broke down with sobs. She
was not discouraged. Soon, more and more people joined in,
and together they raised their voices in supplication for the
end of the war, and the end of our misery. Strengthened by
common bonds, they were ready for the future.

Then Tashkent became the magic, Promised Land. If we
could only get there, everything would be all right. Since the
train moved, we might get there yet. We passed Magnitogorsk,
at the foot of the Ural Mountains. We were passing Cheliabinsk,
and still going east. Nobody talked. People ran out of words.
Any voice would only add to our aggravation.

Night fell, and the train rolled with the same speed. At
midnight it stopped. My mother looked through the window but couldn't see anything. Remembering how the train
was abandoned on the side track near Moscow, she was afraid
that we were abandoned again in the steppes. She hoped
that everybody was asleep. There would be plenty of time to
worry about it in the morning, but sleep eluded her. She lay
there thinking what to do: maybe we should leave the train
and settle here, maybe we had arrived at our destination,
maybe they were sending us to a different *sovhoz* since we
had lost so much time. These thoughts kept her awake, afraid,
and overwhelmed with frustration.

The night was fading away, and she started hearing things.
She thought she heard the song she used to sing as a morning
prayer. This song was very popular, and everybody knew it.
She strained her ears, and the melody was getting stronger.
Everybody was still asleep, for which she was grateful, because
she thought she was losing her mind. Who could be singing it
in Polish? People here didn't even speak Russian. The sound
was getting louder and louder. She even started recognizing
the words. Now she was sure she had lost her mind. She started
a silent prayer, "Please, God, please help me."

She pressed her ears so as not to hear, but now the song was quite clear, and she heard men singing. She started sobbing, and looked out the window. The last shadows of the night disappeared, and in full daylight she saw tents, hundreds of them, with a Polish flag fluttering way above them. Soldiers stood in formation singing the morning prayer. She was overwhelmed with fear that she had lost her mind.

"Everybody, get up! We are back in Poland. There are Polish soldiers all around us. Get up, get up!" She was screaming like mad.

"Have you lost your mind? Polish soldiers in Russia?"

"Get up! Hear them sing!"

By now everybody heard the singing, but were afraid to admit it. They thought they were crazy too.

"Get up! Look out through the window!"

The frightened people crowded to the small window and looked in disbelief.

"No, it can't be true. Where are we?"

"Open the door! Let them know that people are here."

"Should we leave the train, and go to them?"

"Wait, don't leave the train. I don't think it is real."

A group of soldiers approached the train.

"Open the door! We want to talk to you. Don't leave this place until we tell you to do so. There is a typhoid epidemic, and we want to keep it confined."

"Where are we?"

"You are still in Russia, but soon you are going to leave it for good. Now Russia is our ally. England and the United States are helping Russia to beat the Germans. Russia is in a terrible mess and confusion. The Germans are advancing eastward. Russia suffers enormous losses. There is an agreement with Russia that all Polish prisoners of war will be released from prisons and labor camps. They will join Polish forces formed in southern Russia, and their families will be permitted to leave Russia. Just think. Polish forces in Russia. We have been trying to get in touch with all the labor camps to let the people know that they can leave Russia. This is Semipalatinsk. This is a boot camp for young arrivals. We are also trying to intercept as many trains with Polish people as possible, and send them out of Russia. Your machinist was a Pole, who relieved the Russian machinist of his duty in Cheliabinsk. He told the Russian that he was needed to fight for Mother Russia and defend Leningrad."

"There were about three hundred men and boys going ahead of us to Tashkent. Do you know what had happened to them?"

"We had our men posted on all railroad stations to tell people on trains about the amnesty. Your friends may be in this camp, or maybe they went to Palestine, Iraq, or Iran, where most of the soldiers went after training. There are new camps being formed. We are trying to send as many people as possible out of Russia. Now, with England and the United States, we will beat the Germans in no time, and then we can go back to Poland. Russian promises don't mean much. If their luck changes for the better, they will keep us here and send us back to labor camps. So tomorrow, you will leave for Krasnovodsk, where you will cross the Caspian Sea to Pahlevi, which is in Iran, and then you will be free. You will be living in refugee camps under the auspices of United Nations Relief Administration (U.N.R.A.), but it won't be for long. We will win this war soon. Yes, yes, we will be back in Poland soon! Poland is not lost forever while we are still alive."

Tears of joy and hope streamed down the sunken cheeks of the refugees. All the suffering was forgotten. They were ready to offer what was left of their lives for their country.

Later in the morning some ladies representing the Red

Cross arrived, bringing with them cans of condensed milk. With a teaspoon they gave each child a lick. The spoons were licked clean. Each child also received a slice of bread and a small bar of chocolate. In the evening everybody got a full meal. It must have been a miracle, we thought. Why were we saved when so many had perished and many were still in prisons and labor camps and didn't know about the amnesty? People prayed individually and in groups, singing with tears in their eyes and lumps in their throats. They thanked God for the delivery from evil and prayed for mercy and protection.

Our seven cars were connected with the military transport, and we reached Kirmine, the central point from which people left for Krasnovodsk. Kirmine was an extremely large railroad station. The number of trains, and the large numbers of people on them, gave the impression of a large city. Soldiers came to the civilian transports looking for their families and friends. We were allowed to leave our cars to go to the public baths. It was very hot and the people took advantage of this luxury. Some of them took a bath twice a day to wash off the two years of accumulated Russian dirt.

Many families found their loved ones. Some women found their husbands who had been arrested at the beginning of the war. Bronica found her husband, but her joy was very short-lived, as his unit soon left for Iran. Still, just to have seen him alive lifted her spirit. He gave her a bottle of vodka which we later used as medicine. She also found out from him that those who had left Uyma at the beginning of the amnesty had perished.

In our transport, only four people had died. Three of them were children who died of starvation, and a fifteen-year-old boy had fallen under the train. He was carrying a sack of bread to the train when the train started moving. He tried to jump into the car but slipped. His sack fell into the car, but he fell under the train. Nobody knew whether he was killed instantly or not. The train left, and his family never knew the details of his death.

Now we had three meals a day. In addition, we were getting medical care. The intense heat, overcrowding, malnutrition, and lack of hygiene favored the development of typhus, dysentery malaria, tuberculosis, and other pulmonary diseases. Now more people died of epidemics than of starvation. Some families were wiped out completely, and Kirmine got the name of "The Valley of Death."

I was the first in our family to become seriously ill. I had a high fever and coughed all the time. Everybody was looking for some shade while I trembled from cold and tried to stay in the sun. Also, I tried to sleep, but coughing kept me awake. Finally, we had to leave the car to be registered for the transport to Krasnovodsk. We were elated to leave the country of our shame, humiliation, and depravation.

As soon as the Russians got a stronger foothold against the Germans, Stalin stopped all the transports. Those unfortunate Poles who had not been able to leave stayed in the Soviet Union until the end of the war. After the war, they were repatriated to western Poland. Their life didn't change. Often it became worse, because they didn't have the energy to start again.

These were our thoughts as we left for Krasnovodsk:

Goodbye, Tashkent! We will never see you. We will remember your name as a sign which changed our life. During our long journey we thought about you the same way Jews thought of the Promised Land. Providence guided us in your direction so we could be free, and regain our humanity and rise above personal shame and degradation. Goodbye!

CHAPTER SIX

Krasnovodsk

Ocean waves lapping,
Warm sun, azure sky, morning,
Prayer heavenward.

Krasnovodsk is a Russian port on the Caspian Sea. We arrived there on April 1, 1942, when we left our car for good, and stood in line at a soup kitchen. The health workers registered everybody and tried to separate the sick from the rest. My mother wanted to tell them how sick I was, but the lady who registered us quietly urged my mother not to mention my sickness, and to support me as best she could. The Russian hospitals had no medicine. If I entered one I might die and mother might never see me again.

My mother and Bronica supported me. They practically carried me between them. Bronica gave me a gulp of vodka to bring some color to my face.

We moved at a snail's pace toward the harbor. In such a crowd we couldn't see the beginning or the end of the line. After a few hours, we saw a seashore and, a little further, many barges. Boats carried us to the barges. When a barge was full, it took off. Those leaving waved enthusiastically and shouted, "We will meet again in freedom."

We boarded one barge, but there was standing room only. Those near the rails held on to them, the rest bounced from one person to another. People formed a line to the bathroom, and when they left the bathroom, they stood in line again. Fortunately, the sea was calm. Our deck was only a few feet above the water. More aggressive people pushed others aside to sit on the deck and enjoy the night sky.

There was a large room under the deck with many benches. Sick people were directed there. The lucky ones grabbed the benches; the rest spread their blankets on the floor.

As we went farther and farther from shore, some of the people became panicky. They were afraid that, after we reached the open sea, we would be pushed into the water. It wouldn't have been such a great loss. These were only women and children. Most of them were sick skeletons. Fear confused their senses. Some were crying, some were singing, others prayed. Some paced the deck, pushing others out of their way. The most sensible ones went to sleep. They slept on the deck, peaceful with the breath of freedom.

I went down under the deck with the sick. They were moaning, groaning, and hallucinating. One person screamed with pain and fell off a bench. There was no one to help him. He went into an epileptic shock and died. Two men came, carried him to the upper deck, and in everybody's view, threw him into the sea. Not one word was uttered. People clung to life. They reined in their emotions so as not to endanger the threads of life that held them together.

In the evening of the next day, we docked in Pahlevi. We were free! We were in Iran. As passengers got off the barge, they kissed the ground of freedom. The sick were asked to stay on the barge. At the last minute my mother came to pull me out. I crawled behind her and we got off. The barge went back with the sick people. When it reached Krasnovodsk it was empty.

We had a meal and everybody went to take a shower. All our clothing was burned. Before we entered the showers, every hair on our bodies was shaved. After showers every person received a blanket and a piece of clothing.

People were drunk with freedom. They watched the fires consuming the clothes, and when the sparks flew people cheered that Russian lice were burning. Some courageous souls celebrated their freedom by plunging into the sea to swim.

The night brought peace. People covered themselves with their blankets and fell asleep on the beach. In the morning, as far as one could see, were little human bumps all over the beach. The morning sun awoke everyone, and the beach became alive with movement. Just like turtles, people dug themselves out of the sand. Now we could see that there were thousands and thousands of people. Some of them lived in tents. They had been here for over a month. There were military and civilian camps, and also a military hospital with patients in every bed. Those who lived in tents were in the clean section. In two weeks there would be a complete change over. The people in the tents would go to Tehran, and we, after everything we had was burned again, after we were showered and shaved again, would move into the tents.

Among these ant mounds of people there was one spot that attracted everybody's attention. It was a small altar. A priest celebrated a mass. It was Easter, the holiest day in the Catholic religion. "Alleluia, He is Risen!" People knelt, stood, or sat on the sand, and those not strong enough lay prostrated before the altar. They sang repeatedly, "He is Risen." Jesus had risen from death. We had risen from a Russian hell, from shame and degradation. We didn't feel forlorn anymore.

Masses followed one after another all that day. Crowds didn't diminish. People sang their hearts out. As the songs intensified, many broke down with sobs, then started singing again. They felt united and strengthened. Their experiences had unified them, and they now stood strong to testify to the existence of the spirit of brotherhood.

I sat alone and distant, looking at the crowd and trying to participate. I had forgotten all the prayers. It had been the custom in our house to sing religious songs, Christmas carols and psalms. I tried to remember them, but could not. High fever and fatigue made me drowsy. I fell asleep. In my sleep I heard some commotion, noises and laughter. When I opened my eyes I saw the whole family and Bronica's husband wishing each other Happy Easter. Bruno brought us some hard boiled eggs, dates, raisins, and white bread. It was a joyous moment and a very short one. His unit was on its way to Iraq. From then on, all I did was sleep. Mother woke me only to give me something to eat, or when we had to change our place.

While the sun baked us alive, the flies drove us to madness. Iranian merchants trying to sell their goods mingled with the population, but nobody could buy anything. The camp police tried to chase the merchants out because of typhus and dysentery, but they were tenacious and didn't want to leave.

There was no more room in the hospital, so the sick ones stayed in their tents. When somebody died, he was buried right away, so as not to spread the disease.

We started our second two weeks' quarantine. Everything we had was burned again. Showers had only cold water. Children screamed. Showered and shaved, we received some pieces of clothing and moved into the tents. From there, after two weeks, we would go to Tehran.

Our day finally arrived. We boarded military trucks and Iranian buses. The narrow road snaked among the picturesque Elbruz Mountains. When the road turned we glimpsed the deep ravines. The sight frightened us and made us dizzy. For the night we stopped in Reshet, a small oasis. There was a beautiful grove of pomegranate fruit trees. A little farther along was a large building. Many of us bedded there for the night. The rest spread their blankets under the trees and went to sleep lulled by twinkling stars.

We had a room with a large window on the third floor of the building. We sat on the floor and tried to sleep. Bronica complained of severe headache and nausea. She sat on the window sill to get some fresh air, but fainted. Fortunately, she fell toward us. The fall revived her, but she felt so weak she couldn't get up. We carried her downstairs, calling the nurse. Bronica was taken to a bus carrying the sick which served as a hospital. She had typhoid fever. Her fever was so high she was unconscious.

We passed the city of Tehran and on the outskirts of the town we reached the city of tents. There were four different camps. Camp number one was a hospital. We were in camp number two, and tent forty-two. There must have been at least one hundred people in each tent. We spread our blankets on the ground between two other families. Each family left some kind of sign on their blankets, so that in the evening they would know where to go to sleep.

There we started a "normal" life. The children went to school. Classes continued from breakfast till dark, six days a week. We had lost two years, so we had to study very hard to catch up. There were no grades. Groups of children studied together until they reached a certain level. All classes were outdoors. Children sat on bricks in a circle, with a brick on their lap to serve as a desk. Teachers had no books or manuals. As they taught from memory, children tried to memorize everything. Slowly, students progressed to a higher level, depending on their knowledge. Nobody complained.

Every morning, Ema, Michalina, Helena, Josephine, and Thad, with their pencils and note books made from toilet paper, ran to their classes. The girls became Girl Scouts or Brownies. Josephine and Thad went to a catechism class. Josephine tried to include me in all her activities, but I was so weak I could hardly stand up. All the adults worked in every profession to make each camp self-sufficient.

One morning my mother took me to the infirmary. The line was long, so she left me and went back to her work. I sat on a bench and talked in my sleep. After a medical examination I was taken directly to the camp hospital. Before I could enter the hospital tent, I had another cold shower, and my head was shaved again. I was in extreme pain and cried as loud as I could. The nurse wrapped me in my blanket, carried me into the tent, and laid me on a bed.

Every bed in the hospital had a patient in it. Often there were two patients in the same bed. The few doctors and nurses doubled their efforts, but the sheer number of sick people overwhelmed them. They were unable to examine every person. In the same tent there were often patients with typhus, dysentery, and pulmonary diseases. The dead were buried at once. The vacated beds were immediately taken by other patients. Beds had no mattresses or sheets. Each patient came with his own blanket, which served as the mattress and cover.

I was in a bed with another person. I had no idea who that person was. Everybody in this tent had typhus. Some of them had passed the crisis and hoped to leave the hospital soon. During the night I must have been terribly restless, and, I pushed the other person off the bed. In the morning one patient told me that I could be comfortable, because my bed-mate went to another tent. When I asked what was in the other tent, they told me that it was a morgue, full of cadavers.

Each evening the list of the deceased was displayed, and a long line of people read the names. Some left hopeful, others, who found the names of their loved ones, departed sobbing.

One day the nurse came and gave me pajamas. In spite of her pleading, I didn't want to put them on. With my head shaved, and in pajamas, I thought everybody would take me for a boy, and if I died my mother would never find me. I cried and cried. I begged for a nightgown, but there weren't any. It had been a week since I had come to the hospital and I had yet to see a member of my family.

After another medical examination I went to a tent where the patients had pulmonary diseases. Most of the time I was unconscious. Every time the nurse awakened me to give me medicine or something to eat and drink, I cried. I felt that the minute I fell asleep they woke me up again. Actually, I was awakened only once a day.

Once, through my sleep, I heard voices. I opened my eyes and saw a doctor and a nurse standing next to my bed. They talked about something, shook their heads, and the only thing I heard was, "Maybe this will help. Let us try it." I didn't know what happened next, but I felt an excruciating pain in my chest and fell asleep. I found out later that I slept for two weeks, and everybody in the tent had been sure that I would die.

One morning I heard somebody calling my name. I thought it was a dream, but I heard it closer and closer. Opening my eyes, I saw my mother in the entrance to the tent. The

only way to find the sick members of the family was to go
from tent to tent, to call their names, and to look at the ones
who couldn't answer. My mother told me that I had been in
the hospital for a whole month, and that Bronica was in the
same hospital. She had passed the crisis of typhoid, but she
was still very sick with hepatitis and malaria. Michalina and
Helena were sick in the hospital but could leave soon. Ema
had been in the hospital for two weeks but was well now.
Only Josephine and Thad missed the hospital. They were all
right and attended school.

The British government promised to resettle the refugees
in their colonies. As people got better, transports went to
Kenya, Rhodesia, Tanganyika, and India. The refugees still
lived in camps, but it was one family to a tent or, later, to a
small hut. There were several thousand refugees in each loca-
tion. All children went to school. Adults worked in education,
human services, kitchen, and laundry. The most enterprising
could live in the cities and find work there. Young boys joined
the military academy and went to Egypt or Palestine. Many
young girls also joined the academy and left for Palestine.
Orphans and children who needed special care went to Isfahan.
Our family stayed in Tehran because two of us were still in
the hospital.

Slowly, I was regaining my health. As I slept less, I got
acquainted with other patients in the tent. There were ten of
us of varying ages. On the next bed was a small, very sick
girl. She talked feverishly in her sleep and cried to go home.
Her mother came twice a day; then both of them cried.
Finally, her mother promised to take her home the next day.

In the morning we ate our breakfast. I sat on the floor with
a bowl of porridge, thinking I had never eaten anything so
delicious. I asked for more porridge, and the nurse gladly

gave it to me, and said that I must really feel good. We also had bread and butter and a cup of cocoa.

The little girl took a sip of cocoa and got a terrible hiccup. This progressed into a convulsion, and a few minutes later she was dead. By the time her mother arrived, the girl was in the morgue, ready for burial.

I didn't feel sorry for the old people when they died. They had lived their lives and suffered a lot, but thinking of the little girl, my eyes flooded with tears. Others felt the same way. We cried as if she had been a member of the family. Such a small child, but she had suffered so much in her short life. When everything had changed for the better, when she had everything to live for, her life was cut short. We cried for her, for ourselves, for our families and for all the injustices done to us. We had been taken from our homes, worked to death; we had lost everything we had, and lost many friends and loved ones. The war had broken our nests, scattering their inhabitants all over the world. Would the broken nests ever be whole? Though we were saved, what did we have to look forward to?

We were hardened by death and suffering, but now we cried unashamedly. The rest of the day was very quiet, interrupted only by the loud clearing of throats and blowing of noses. We realized that we had to get control of our lives, but the future looked frightening, and we were scared to think about it.

As the days went on, the number of patients in the hospital decreased. Those that were too sick died, and the rest slowly regained their health. The number of deceased exceeded those who were alive. The hospital moved from the outskirts of Tehran into the city. The sickest patients were doctored in the buildings. Those who were not so sick, and those who would be discharged shortly, stayed in the tents.

Bronica was in the building. That meant that her stay in the hospital was going to be long. I was much better, so I stayed in the tent.

Our tent had about eighty patients of all ages and both sexes. It was terribly hot during the day. During the night the sick moaned and groaned. Nearby, the hyenas and jackals howled all night long. I trembled with fear and had no rest. Instead of getting better I was getting worse. I had to do something to leave the hospital. One patient told me that if my fever stayed normal for a week I might be discharged. I tried to cheat, but apparently I was still too sick.

After a few weeks I felt better and decided to visit Bronica. I had become used to my pajamas. Barefoot, I roamed through the hospital buildings and tents.

We had plenty to eat, in the hospital, but when I visited Bronica she complained of being hungry. The next time I wanted to surprise her. I brought her a few meat balls in my pajama leggings. She took a bite and said that they were very good, but before she had a chance to take a second bite, she was writhing in convulsions from pain. My good intentions prolonged her stay in the hospital by a whole month.

Finally I was well enough to leave the hospital. I had entered the hospital at the beginning of April and it was now June 20. My hair had grown about an inch and looked like barbed wire. I looked like a scarecrow wearing a dress and sandals. Leaving the hospital, I was afraid that I might not find our tent. The only thing I remembered was a number, but whether it was the row or the tent number I had forgotten.

The military truck dropped the discharged patients at the entrance to the camp. Looking at the multitude of tents, I felt lost. Where should I start? I looked into every tent, walked through them, and tried to recognize something familiar.

Fortunately I started from the right end, because after a short while I found our tent and Mother in it. Mother didn't recognize me. She had to look at me for a long time before she could admit that I was one of hers.

That day was the feast of St. John. It was also a school break. Teachers and children worked very hard to prepare a show to let people enjoy themselves. Small girls were dressed in green-colored undershirts. Red paper flowers were pinned to the straps and the belt had a large bow. More flowers were pinned to the flounce at the bottom. The little girls wore garlands of paper flowers on their heads. It was difficult to keep those garlands in place because their hair was still very short. These little girls were to represent butterflies, flowers, and pages in the garden of a princess. Josephine was among them. She danced with verve. Late into the night the children sang and danced. The audience applauded, and the echo repeated the applause, increasing the enthusiasm of the people.

The show was over, but people stayed. They sang, laughed, and enjoyed themselves. Since it was Saturday, they had a night out. Small and large groups went to the pool, swam, and danced. They were afraid to stop, thinking that it might be a dream which could be very rudely interrupted. Sad memories were pushed away. People tried to fill every minute with the joy of life, preparing to meet their "tomorrow."

Sunday morning we drove into the mountains. Children and adults climbed onto the trucks, and off we went. Everybody sang. The songs were beautiful, full of life and promise. One was lovelier than the others. I listened intently, trying to remember the words. The melody changed, and the words were different, so I just opened my mouth and listened.

This was my first time in the mountains. The singing birds, the murmur of the brooks, the green bushes, and the trees

engulfed us with their magnificence. Children scattered all
over. Happy screams and laughter resounded everywhere.
Some daring souls plunged into the cold mountain streams.
Fun and joy were in abundance. By dusk we got on our trucks
and headed back.

The next morning I got up with an excruciating headache
and high fever from sunstroke. That had been my first full
day in the sun in many months. With my hair so short, I should
have worn a hat. I cried and was afraid that I might have to go
to the hospital. My mother took me to the doctor, who gave
me strict orders not to go out into the sun, to stay in the tent,
and to rest. I stayed in all day long. In the evening Josephine
took me to her catechism class and Brownie meeting.

One evening, young children put on a show for the whole
camp. They danced folk dances, sang many songs, and
recited poems. There was a skit depicting the death of Hitler
and his acceptance into hell. The multitude of devils in the
entourage prepared a bath for Hitler from the blood of the
murdered children. When Hitler protested that he was inno-
cent, the audience was outraged and everybody screamed,
"Kill him! Kill that bastard! He was the reason for our suffering." People, in their minds, were back at the beginning of
the war, trampled by German boots, bombed by German
planes, and shot without mercy. This skit had reminded them
of the cruelty and brutality of the German barbarians. They
felt ready to kill, to get rid of this cancer of humanity. The
scene was ugly and violent in emotion. Thoughts and memories that everybody had tried to forget had come back. To
save the show and to quench the riot, children raised their
voices in the national anthem. Soon the angry voices hushed.
Everybody stood at attention, listening with great emotion.
"Poland is not dead, as long as we are alive."

The camps grew smaller as people left for other resettlement centers. There were many orphans in our camp. Authorities tried to save as many children as possible. They chose Isfahan as the next site because of its good climate, its history, its building facilities, and its distance far away from Russia. They had sent several transports of children there already, and another transport was soon to leave. Michalina, Helena, and Josephine were among the children to go. I wanted to go too, but the day before they left I changed my mind and cried the whole night, not consoled at the thought of separation. Mother tried to persuade me, that I could join them later. Somehow, I was afraid that if they went, I wouldn't see them again. If I went, I wouldn't see my mother again either.

In the morning, all the departing children received their provision of food and boarded the trucks. As the motors started, I jumped in and went with my sisters to Isfahan.

I didn't know how many children were on the truck, but it was pretty crowded. Some of us sat on the floor, other children stood. Children looked at the scenery and sang. I had learned many songs, so now I could sing with everybody else. Late in the afternoon, we stopped at the small oasis named Dylizhan. We sat under the palms and listened to the splashes of water. It seemed like such a frivolous little sound, but its cheerfulness was very refreshing.

There was a small shop where we could get some tea. Children took out their food. My sisters shared their food with me. By night we sat under the palms, wrapped ourselves in our blankets, and fell asleep.

As our trucks drove through the Elbruz Mountains we saw the snow-covered peak of Demavend. Not very high as heights go, but we thought it reached heaven. At noon we stopped for a short rest at the oasis called Qume. Under the shade of pomegranates, we ate our lunch of bread, hard boiled eggs, and dates. We drank water from a spring, and washed the dust from our faces.

Late in the afternoon our trucks entered Isfahan. We passed small huts on dirt streets. A little farther we saw lovely buildings among the trees, and above them, reflecting the sun, were the blue and gold cupolas of many mosques. We passed downtown with its paved, wide streets full of flowers and shops. The buildings were surrounded by high walls.

We reached our destination. We hoped that, in this good climate, we would be able to regain our health, become strong, and start a normal life. Maybe we would even live like normal children of our age. We would go to school and wouldn't have to worry about our daily needs. We might even have some fun, but would we know how to play?

CHAPTER SEVEN

Isfahan

Smiling children laugh,
Spring into fall, bashful joy,
Hope, promise, future.

I sfahan spreads out in the valley between the Elbruz and
Zagros Mountains. Once, it was the capital of Persia. The
splendor of the past could be seen in the architecture of its
buildings, which were large and spread all over the town.
Long ago they must have been the mansions of very rich
people. Now these empty buildings were rented and turned
into dormitories for Polish children.

The buildings were self sufficient. Children were grouped
according to age. Each building housed from eighty to three
hundred and fifty children. The mothers were employed so
that they could be with the youngest children.

Michalina, Helena, Josephine, and I went to building number nine. It was an elementary school. Each of us was in a
different grade and room. Our rooms were our bedrooms,
classrooms, dining room, and laundry room. In the morning, we folded our bedding neatly into a square at the head
of the cot, so the other end of the cot could be used for a

different purpose. There were no chairs or tables, so our beds served many functions. There was no problem with discipline. Cleanliness was exemplary.

In our dormitory we had many girls who were cadets. Still observing the old rules, every morning they woke everybody up for exercise and drill. Most of us had never heard of a drill, but cadets were persistent, so we had no choice but to participate.

Every grade had a home-room teacher, who very often was a mother, a father, or a sister. They taught us, helped us with our laundry, braided our hair, cared for us when we were sick, and told us bedtime stories. When they found a book, they read it to us. They were in their twenties and had suffered just as much as most of us, yet they cared for us unselfishly, and tried to make our life as normal as possible.

The school stayed in session year-round, from eight in the morning until four in the afternoon, and half a day on Saturday. We had much catching up to do but nobody complained.

There were twenty buildings rented for resettlement facilities throughout the town. Two of the dormitories were very special, each housing one hundred children. One dormitory was run by the sisters of Charity. The children in that building were supported by the Pope. They were beautifully dressed in light blue dresses with white collars, light checkered coats, good shoes, and blue berets. They studied French, music, and piano. Most of them were orphans, and had been the first to arrive in Isfahan. Their dormitory had nearby a beautiful church in which the mass was celebrated every day. Sunday, children from other dormitories attended the mass in their church. The group of girls, and I among them, received our first communion there.

This was a beautiful ceremony prepared by the Sisters

of Charity. After the mass we had breakfast with the sisters and a short trip to the Persian market. In the evening we had a show prepared by the girls in the dormitory. The events of that day were heart-warming and memorable. It took us a long time to find out where the sisters had found so many white dresses and veils. Much later there was a request for new petticoats for the sisters and new sheers for the windows.

Not far from this dormitory was another one for one hundred orphaned boys who enjoyed the same caring atmosphere under the fatherly eyes of priests. The boys wore navy blue pants and shorts, white shirts, and nice black shoes. The rest of the children didn't have as much, but they had no reason to complain either.

Each dormitory had Brownies, or Girl or Boy Scouts. Our uniforms were white. We also had khaki and gray uniforms, and sandals. That was the extent of our wardrobe. Since each dormitory had only one iron, we had to use our imagination on how to look presentable. After we washed our uniforms, we spread them on our mattresses and covered them with the sheet. Overnight, the weight of our body dried and pressed the uniform. Later, when too many of us developed colds from the dampness, our supervisors saw to it that we didn't do this again.

Each dormitory, just as every building in Isfahan, was surrounded by a high wall. We had no money and there was no need for us to go to town.

This self-sufficiency was very confining to us. Though downtown was right behind the gate, we seldom left our premises. Only on Sunday, in formation, we did leave the building to attend mass. As we marched singing, small Persian boys made their own formations and either followed us, or marched next to us. They also learned the words and melodies of our songs very quickly, and sang with us. We found it very amusing. Every Sunday we tried to sing a different song, but the little boys had no problem learning them quickly.

A month after our arrival my mother arrived with Thad in Isfahan. Since Thad was still small, both of them stayed in the same building. Thad went to school and mother worked in the laundry.

Bronica left the hospital, but was still too weak to take any job, so Ema stayed with her in the camp near Tehran. Ema went to school while Bronica recuperated. One year later both of them came to Isfahan. Bronica got a job taking care of small children, while Ema attended a vocational school. We were together again. By together, I mean that during the holidays we all could go to our mother's building and spend holidays there. Otherwise, we were in four different dormitories.

There were very few occasions for us to interact with the local population. Any time we went out, we went in a large group under the supervision of our teachers. For entertainment we went to different dormitories for shows, dances, songs, or campfires. We visited the Persian market and admired gold, silver, copper, and brass items. We also visited several textile shops and marveled at the intricate patterns and methods of carpet-making. Each pattern was a closely guarded secret and couldn't be repeated. Young girls with nimble fingers wove different colors and as we watched they were oblivious to our attention.

The high point of our cultural education was visiting mosques. We had to have special permission to enter them. There were many of them, and one was of surpassing beauty. Architecturally they were similar to each other, but the mosaic of patterns and colors was more beautiful than one could imagine. The mosques were cool and spacious. The only decorations were the exquisite carpets on the floor. When Moslems prayed, they knelt on the rugs. The inside of the mosque was void of any statues or other articles of faith. When they prayed, the worshipers turned toward Mecca.

Josephine, Helena, and I lived in dormitory number nine, on the main street in Isfahan, next to the mosque that had previously been attended by the royal family. My bedroom was on the second floor with a view of the main street. I loved to wake up at sunrise. The cupolas of the mosques shone in the sun reflecting a rainbow of colors. Caravans of camels walked slowly down the street, little bells jingled at their necks, and Bedouins with whips urged them to go faster. Camels' hooves rapped on the street. These noises didn't interfere with the Muezzin's call to prayer. The sounds harmonized with awakening life.

In this healthy and beautiful atmosphere time went very fast. Before we knew it, two years passed. The older girls graduated from high school and left for Egypt or Palestine to continue their education. The rest of us studied hard, six days a week. Our teachers tried to teach us everything that might be useful to us in our future lives. They wanted to make us as independent as possible.

A new transport of children arrived in Isfahan. In this good climate they would quickly regain their health. Our buildings were filled. During resettlement, a large group of orphaned children went to New Zealand, India, and Mexico. Orphans in Mexico lived in convents. After the war, most of them emigrated to the United States. Our family was on the list to go to New Zealand, but in such a large family as ours there was always someone in the hospital. For now we stayed in Isfahan.

Among the orphans leaving for New Zealand was one little boy by the name of Adolf Niziol, the same last name as ours. My mother, convinced that he was relative on my father's side, wanted him to stay as part of our family. She even asked the authorities not to send him to New Zealand, saying she would take care of him. They rudely told her that she should take care of her seven children, and Adolf was sent to New Zealand.

Our food came from Tehran. Several times the drivers complained that halfway between Tehran and Isfahan, bands of robbers attacked the transports and stole everything. The drivers didn't suffer any physical abuse. Again we had no food, and we were very hungry. The bread we had during this time was made with corn flour, filled with so many bugs that we didn't know whether we ate the bread with the bugs, or the bugs with the bread. For dinner everyday we ate potatoes and onions. Children were afraid that they would starve again. They became withdrawn and cried a lot. After the authorities investigated these mysterious robberies and changed drivers, the robberies didn't happen again, and there was no shortage of food.

With the coming of spring many children developed eye diseases. It became necessary to isolate the sick children so as not to spread the disease, and to keep the sick children close to the doctor and hospital. Since building nine met all the requirements, all the sick children went there, and the healthy ones had to go to different dormitories.

Helena was sick, so Josephine and I had to go. I went with a large group to building number six, called Julfa, which was on the outskirts of Isfahan. It was the Armenian community. Josephine stayed in number nine until room was found for her in one of the other dormitories.

Number six dormitory was the largest one. There were three bedrooms that housed sixty children each. This was a two-story building with a large basement. Once, it must have been a magnificent mansion. There were large balconies on the second floor. We loved to sit out there and look at the mountains. In the front of the building the grounds were bordered by evergreens. We used this place for our morning exercise and different games. We had electric lights in our rooms and dirt floors. These floors must once have been covered by Persian carpets.

One day our curiosity forced us to find out what was in the basement. We found a window, which we managed to open and, one by one, we descended into the darkness. When our eyes became accustomed to the darkness, we saw many big barrels. We were sure that this must have been the hiding place of Ali Baba and his forty thieves.

Back of the building were grape vines and a church. The Armenians living in Julfa were Catholics of the Maronite rite. It was very fortunate for us, because we had a church in our back yard. The Armenians not only welcomed us to their church, but their pastor, Father Leon, also became fluent in the Polish language. He became our confessor, celebrated our masses, said the homily in Polish, and sang all our religious songs with us.

For the Corpus Christi celebration, he translated the Polish song "Immaculate Mary" into the Armenian language, and there was a procession to the church with one hundred Polish and one hundred Armenian girls. We were dressed in navy blue, pleated skirts and white blouses, with blue ribbons in our hair. We walked together singing "Immaculate Mary" once in Armenian and then in Polish. The entire Armenian Parish was in church, and they liked our procession very much.

Father Leon also became our teacher of religion. Though he had his own parish, we always knew where to find him. A high wall surrounded both his church and our dormitory.

I was the only one from our family in this dormitory. This was the first time that I didn't have to worry about taking care of a younger sister or brother. One afternoon the gate opened and a rickshaw entered the yard. I was surprised to see Josephine in the company of the headmistress from dormitory nine. The headmistress said that after I had left the dormitory, Josephine cried all the time and didn't want to eat or do anything. The headmistress had no choice but to bring her to Julfa to join me. From this time on we were always together.

Now two of us were in Julfa. Helena was left in building nine. It seemed to us that as soon as we would get used to one dormitory, we would have to move. More and more children reached high school level; when children reached the appropriate grade level they were grouped accordingly. When we had to move from one dormitory to another, we packed all our possessions from under our pillows, and marched to another dormitory.

Our life became routine. Sometimes we got a longer break, and then children went to visit their mothers, attended the Scout camp, or caught up on their studies.

Once, we received news that Shah Reza Pahlevi was coming to Isfahan with his family, to his summer residence. Our faculty was energized and decided to organize a show for such a distinguished person, to show him our gratitude for accepting us into his very hospitable country. The faculty chose a short operetta "Krakowskie Wesele," which had many folk dances and songs. Our activities increased. From early morning to late afternoon we rehearsed dances and songs. Our music teacher got in touch with the Persian Orchestra and rehearsed the music for the show with them.

Four of us sang in a choir which was going to perform for the Shah of Iran. We rehearsed all day and all evening long, until songs put us to sleep. The day before the performance we received white uniforms with navy blue ribbons for our hair, which by now was long and could be braided. We guarded our uniforms from the smallest specks of dust, polished our sandals, and washed our hair for the tenth time. That morning we had a full-dress rehearsal. Our teacher, though very pleased, was extremely nervous. We were going to the Shah's residence to entertain him.

The day of the performance we boarded the trucks lined up outside the gate, and sang all the way to the Shah's residence. The event took place in the theater inside his palace. We expected the Shah to be sitting on the peacock throne with a crown on his head, but nobody was in the theater when we entered. It gave us a little time to look around and admire the wealth and luxury of the palace. We took our place on the balcony across from the stage. Slowly the theater started to fill with dignitaries from Isfahan and the Shah's palace. The orchestra took its place and softly played excerpts from the show. Then, there was silence. In the company of his wife and two daughters, the Shah entered the theater. Everybody rose and applauded. His entourage followed. The royal family, the entourage, and the attending public projected extreme wealth. Their jewels reflected in the light. We couldn't take our eyes off the Shah's two daughters. They wore the most beautiful dresses we had ever seen.

While the orchestra played the national anthem, everybody turned toward the Shah. After he sat down, the show started with the "Polonaise." It was beautiful when the dancers bowed to the royal family, then the audience, and continued with the dance. The Shah and the audience applauded with gusto, the orchestra played with verve, and the turbaned heads of players swayed with the beat of the music. After the "Polonaise" there was "Mazurka," "Oberek," "Kujawiak," "Krakowiak," and even one Persian dance. Our choir sang during the changes of scenery. Judging by the applause of the audience and their requests for encores, we were sure that they liked the singing very much.

After the show, the Shah came to our group, thanked us graciously for an enjoyable evening, and invited us to visit the rest of the palace. It was called the palace of forty columns. There were only twenty columns, ten on each side of the pool, but they were reflected in the water and we counted forty of them.

This was a very important event in our lives. For the longest time we talked, talked and talked about the Shah, about the Shah, about the Shah ... about his daughters. We even tried to imagine that the Shah might take care of us.

Another big event was an earthquake. We were awakened by a strong shake, and we felt as if we were on a large swing. We didn't suffer any damage, but small villages in the mountains were destroyed and there were some casualties. Our faculty thought that we could organize a show for the people of Isfahan and send the proceeds to the villagers. Some members of the faculty knew how to play musical instruments, so they became our orchestra. Since dormitory number six was the largest one, that is where the show was going to be presented. In the corner, a stage was attached to the building. It was constructed of boards supported by the barrels left by "Ali Baba and his forty thieves." There was no curtain, but the walls were decorated with paper flowers and branches of trees. The barrels were camouflaged by evergreens. One dance was set by a river, so blue paper was placed on the stage to snake like a river. Dancers still had their costumes from the Shah's show, so everything was organized very quickly.

The show started on a Saturday afternoon. A large number of the local population filled our courtyard to capacity. The audience loved the dances and applauded vigorously. They asked for two or three encores after every dance. They liked it so much and were so enthusiastic, that very often some of them jumped on the stage and wanted to learn the steps.

We had performances every day for a whole week, and the place was always packed. Some people came every day. They had learned the steps and while the dancers danced on the stage, they danced among the public. They also learned our songs very quickly and sang with us. They loved "Mazurka," and screamed for encores. Sometimes they kept the dancers on one dance so long that the programs weren't completed. Our exhausted dancers were given a vacation from their classes for the entire week.

The show was a tremendous success, not only financially, but it was the first time we had mingled with the local population. Now they wanted to participate in all our events, and sing all our songs. They seemed to have learned by osmosis, and from this time on there was no problem buying anything. Every shopkeeper knew Polish. There was one song, "Wrocimy tam," which was important for us refugees. It was full of emotion and longing for our homes and lost childhood. Somehow, the Iranians loved this song very much and sang it incessantly.

Our life, though very regimented, was peaceful and safe. We were not oblivious to the war, but it seemed so far away. We were certain that Hitler would be defeated, that Poland would regain its independence, and we would go home. We tried to learn as much as possible, so that when we would get home, we could work.

We heard that the Polish forces fought on Monte Cassino and that the Germans suffered a decisive defeat. Our hopes soared. Any defeat of Germany was a great success for humanity. That brutal nation lacked conscience, compassion, and understanding of human nature. Their bestial crimes will be remembered as monuments to their culture.

Though we were far away from the war, whatever happened on the front affected our future. The war was where

our future would be decided. Our stay in Iran was temporary, and at the war's end we would have to leave. We were
almost sure that Hitler would be crushed, but how to get rid
of Stalin? Russia had invaded Poland two weeks after Germany crushed the Polish forces. It was difficult not to be
aware of history and everything that was happening during
the war when it concerned you personally.

Every week we would gather in the library to listen to the
Polish radio news from London. We sat transfixed waiting for
the first sounds of "Water Music." Soon the music faded and
we heard knocks, then we heard: "Tu mowi Londyn." (This is
London). We were all ears. Though the news was scanty and
fragmented, we learned about the Yalta Conference. The
United States, England, and Russia were allies. Polish forces
were fighting together with the British in Tobruk, in the battle
of Britain, in Italy and in Germany. Surely, when Hitler was
defeated, Poland would be free.

Our teachers tried to learn about the Yalta Conference from
French, English, Iranian, and Arabic friends. What they
learned, they conveyed to us. The whole eastern part of
Poland, one third of Poland, was given to Russia. All the Poles
in that region who had been deported to Russia in 1940, in
February, April, and June, had no Poland to return to.

After the Yalta Conference, the Polish Government in
exile in London lost support and recognition from Britain
and the United States. All Polish people, wherever they were,
were asked by the puppet government established by Stalin
to come back to Poland-Russia. Also, the British government
withdrew its support of Polish refugees. This humanitarian
function was taken over by "UNRA," the United Nations
Organization for Refugee Resettlement, and later by "IRO,"
the International Relief Organization.

The Polish delegation from London sent a letter to the

United States President, Franklin D. Roosevelt, to intervene with Stalin about Galicia, without this province and its industry Poland would be extremely handicapped. Galicia was the southern part of Poland. It was rich in natural resources, including oil. Poland depended heavily on these resources, and Stalin was going to steal them from Poland.

Galicia is also the name of a region in Spain. Apparently Roosevelt had never heard of the Polish Galicia. When Roosevelt mentioned Galicia, and said he didn't understand why Poland wanted to include that part of Spain in its borders, Stalin said, "I told you, those Poles are very greedy people." Politicians very seldom sin on the side of knowledge. This gem of information about the statesmanship of those who were ruling the world was later related to the Polish delegation by one of the participants of the Yalta conference.

We felt betrayed. We had had such high hopes. When youngsters had reached their eighteen birthday they had joined the cadets to prepare for the army, to fight for freedom. We found ourselves in a terrible dilemma. If we returned to our homes, we were returning to Russia, which meant death and starvation. We had no idea about the politics, but now we had become stateless, political refugees. Our family had nowhere to go, nor anybody to go to. We could go to my mother's family, but we had never heard from them, and we didn't know if any of them had survived the war. The only choice we had was to stay and see what the future would bring. Many families decided to return to Poland in hopes of joining their relatives and regaining their homes.

At this time Mother was living with two other women in a small room. Often on Sunday or on other holidays, the children went to visit their mothers. In the evening, the beds were pushed together and, like sardines, children and mothers crowded on them. The rest slept on the floor. Before we went to sleep, we always had a little show. Children showed off for their mothers. They sang, danced, and recited poems. Mothers applauded enthusiastically and praised their efforts.

Often, the high point of our entertainment was the song sung by Theresa P. She was only seven years old. A beautiful girl, with long, blond, curly hair, big blue eyes, and very black eyelashes and brows. She looked like a doll and everybody loved her.

One of Theresa's great pleasures was to look through her mother's possessions. She loved to take all the things out of her mother's suitcase, touch each item with reverence, and fold it delicately. Her mother's possessions were few. Nevertheless, Theresa, mindful of Russian poverty, considered them great treasures. She took the things out one at the time, spread them on the bed, and looked at them with great pleasure. Then she folded them gently, putting them back into the suitcase. Adults remembered this well. With the first money they earned, they bought small suitcases in which to stash their possessions. Also, they wanted to be ready for any eventuality.

It was the same with food. We had enough to eat. There was no reason to worry about the lack of food, but after every meal people saved a few slices of bread "for later." This "later" gnawed on their minds. They didn't talk about it, but the fear in their eyes was ever-present.

Our material conditions improved. Besides room and board, we children received pocket money of five rials. Ten walnuts cost one rial, but this was the first money I ever had for my own use. I suddenly felt very rich. I could spend all five rials for my needs. I bought a toothbrush, tooth-paste, ribbons for my hair, and a note book. I dreamed of buying a suitcase, but I considered it a luxury out of my reach. Everything I had, I kept under my pillow.

Our Christmases, until now, had passed uneventfully, but the Christmas of 1944 was very memorable. Every child received a present from Santa Claus. All the presents looked exactly the same. Each child received a tube of tooth-paste, a mixture of nuts and raisins called *kish-mish*, some hard candy and a game, dominos or checkers. What a treat! Who would have thought about us?

We children ate our candy right away and wanted more sweets. The sweetness of the toothpaste was very tempting, and the whole pleasure ended with stomach ache and a night interrupted by bathroom races.

We were going to have a longer break in our school year and we called it a vacation. Since I was a Girl Scout, I went to a Scout camp. I loved to go to the camp. It was run by the Scouts who had been already leaders in scouting before the war. They organized our camps very well. The camps were not only recreational, but also very educational. Every day we spent a few hours on instructional subjects, then exercise, swimming, volleyball, and sometimes a trip to town to visit historical sites.

Once, we went to see a beautiful and extraordinary mosque. It had exquisite mosaic in blue and gold. Stairs led to the top of the cupola. When we reached the top, we formed two groups, and took turns jumping across the floor. When one group jumped, the other one stood still. As we jumped, the whole mosque swayed in the direction of the jump. We became dizzy, but there were no signs of damage to the mosque. The architects must have been very smart. They knew how to build in a region where there were frequent earthquakes. We had so much fun, we tried this procedure a few more times.

Evening hours at camp were the most enjoyable. The Scouts gathered by a campfire. We gave short reports of the most important things we had done during the day. We selected a Scout's deed that we considered the most humane, and songs followed. The campfire put light into our lives. From this fire we took so much energy and light that we could have illuminated the darkest night.

There was so much happiness and closeness that we wanted the camp to be extended indefinitely. Unfortunately, all things end. We had to get ready for school.

After transport of children left for Africa, it was necessary to regroup. Thad was transferred to a different dormitory, where he was away from a family member for the first time. Once, while playing with a group of boys, they climbed a tree that was full of pods. They thought the pods were string beans. The pods were sweet in taste, so each of them ate a few. In a few minutes they started screaming with pain and fainted. They were rushed to the hospital. There was a strong possibility they might die. They were poisoned. All night they moaned, unconscious. The next day they showed some improvement, but they didn't recover until a month later.

We were called to a general assembly, where we found out that the war was over. This should have been the most joyous news, and we should have celebrated. Instead, we were frightened and asked, "What should we do?"

We were all older and stronger. I felt sure we could tackle any job, but now our mother became sick. Before, she had never had time to be sick, but now, finally, everything caught up with her. The knowledge that the war was over, and that we had nowhere to go, put her into a great depression. She became terribly weak. She stayed in bed all day long, not uttering a word. If anyone spoke to her, she pretended she was asleep. She never asked for food or water. Though she went to the hospital, nothing changed, except that she was left alone more often. We took turns visiting her, but she stayed in bed and didn't want to talk. Her nurse told us that it would be much better for our mother to return to her old room. If she were among people she knew, it might help her more than staying in the hospital.

Mother left the hospital. We received a message that all Poles would leave Isfahan, because there was a war in the Middle East. The Jews were fighting with the Arabs to establish a free Jewish state.

My mother had to put her problems aside because soon we would be leaving this hospitable country. We would remember those four years spent in Persia with great affection. We experienced there a revival of our souls and bodies. Even though high walls were between us and the Iranians, we had found them to be a gracious and hospitable people.

There had been very little social exchange between us and the Persians, but when they saw us leaving, they went from one building to another, sang our songs, and pleaded with us to stay. They couldn't understand why we had to go. Many of them proposed marriage, but there were no takers.

The Russians had liberated us from everything, even, many thousands, from life itself. In the atmosphere of kindness and hospitality, we managed to forget our suffering, hunger, deprivation, begging, and looking for scraps of food on Moscow's streets. The visit with the Shah of Persia (now Iran) had been the high point in our lives. We would cherish the memory forever. We said goodbye and were confident that, with God's help, we would be able to handle our future.

Chapter Eight

Farewell Persia

Flowers, summer, fall,
Laughter, sunshine, rainbow, sky.
Family, home, joy!

The first transport was ready in September 1946. We were not sure where we were going. We had an idea that eventually we would go to Lebanon. Meanwhile, we went to Ahvaz, which is a seaport on the Persian Gulf.

Our family left in the last transport. Boarding the trucks, we traveled the same road which had brought us to Isfahan four years ago. Our first stop was Qum, where, in the American camp, we stayed the whole day. When we had stopped in Qum in 1942, there had been no Americans there. Now they had a beautiful camp and they treated us to two meals. In the afternoon they showed us a film. In the evening they transported us to the railroad station.

Thad had no recollection of trains or railroads. When he heard the approaching train, he was extremely frightened. He cried and tried to run away from the oncoming monster. We ran after him and tried to tell him that the train wouldn't hurt him.

We boarded the train. It was a passenger train, but the wooden benches were hard, and too narrow for comfort. Some of us sat on the floor. Others walked up and down through the cars. Some small children climbed up on the shelves and went to sleep.

The transports were designed in such a way as not to interrupt schooling. Many grades traveled with their teachers, so it was only natural for teachers to teach. Every day in the middle of the car the children sat on the floor and teachers conducted lessons. We called it a traveling school.

In our traveling rations we received, among other things, toilet paper. We used it in the classroom to take notes, do our homework, and write essays, letters, and diaries. Only after all these other functions, was it used for the intended purpose.

It took us four and a half days to reach Ahvaz, where we had new experiences. We lived in large stables. There were about ten of them. One stable had hot baths and showers. The stables were so huge, they must have housed at least ten thousand horses. The stables had electric lights, cement floors, and extremely high ceilings. They were clean, spacious, and cool, and the walls were dotted with mangers. Lucky were the families who were next to the mangers, because small children used them for beds. They were also used for storage.

The temperature in Ahvaz stayed over 100 degrees for the better part of the year. People called it hell. It was dangerous to be out in the sun between eleven and four. The stables were cool, and we could take as many showers as we wanted. There were also two swimming pools, but no lockers. We had to leave our clothes on the edge of the pool. Often the clothes were stolen. Since we didn't have many changes of clothing, we decided we preferred to take showers.

In Ahvaz we met people from Tehran and Isfahan, and Poles who had lived there since 1942. There were also American, English, and Indian military camps. The Poles who lived in Ahvaz worked in the camps, and were very well off. They were also well dressed. In comparison to them, we looked like beggars.

We were given a space in the middle row. We spread our blankets on a little deck. The rest of our possessions served as pillows. The cool night gave us some relief from the intense heat.

On Saturday and Sunday evenings, an American film crew came with outdoor movies. Everybody was welcome, including the local population. For them, the film characters were very real. If there was an episode where the police chased a robber or a murderer, they also took off in pursuit. They chased until the picture disappeared. Coming back, they wanted to know what had happened.

We went to school in double shifts. From six in the morning until eleven, the school was for children who had lived there the longest time. From four in the afternoon until nine in the evening, the school was for children who had arrived recently. Everything went smoothly. Many morning students left notes for afternoon students, and in this way many friendships were formed.

Next to our stables were American and Indian camps. Every morning at four, an Indian soldier played a beautiful march for reveille. The melody was strong, yet very tranquil. Somehow, it energized us, filling our stables with confidence and joy. I learned to love it and anxiously waited to hear the reveille from the Indian camp. Many years later I found out that the music was the "Triumphal March" from *Aida*.

The three months in Ahvaz passed quickly. At the end of November we were on the move again. Trucks carried us toward Iraq. Two days later we crossed the border from Iran to Iraq. Those years in Iran would be remembered by us fondly. To me, Iran was like a good sanatorium after a grave illness.

Our first stop in Iraq was Basra, which lies at the delta of the Euphrates River. In a park of palm trees and flowers we ate our breakfast. After a short rest we entered the valley between the Euphrates and Tigris. We felt as if we were in heaven. After all, this was supposed to be the biblical Garden of Eden. The beauty of this valley is difficult to describe: a great profusion of flowers, palms along the rivers, blue waters visible between the trees. Sometimes, we met a camel caravan led by Arabs with turbans on their heads. Our trucks looked like ugly intruders in this tranquil beauty. We admired the beautiful valley and tried to remember as much as possible.

Our next stop was Baghdad where we stopped for the night in an American camp. This was a transient camp. Many Polish soldiers went through it on their way to Palestine, Egypt, and Italy. In the evening many people went to Baghdad to admire the hanging gardens, look at the mosques, and visit the marketplace. They came back exulting in the beauty and the memorable experiences. The next evening we boarded the train. Through palm forests and steppes, we snaked through the desert.

The benches were very hard and there was not enough room to lie down. In the morning our teacher decided to have a regular class. There were no objections, and children eagerly took their seats on the floor.

We had no visa to travel through Turkey or Syria, so on the border of Iraq-Turkey, we changed to cargo cars, twenty to a car. There were no seats or decks, but the floor was

covered with straw. We felt a great relief and stretched out
on the straw. The opening in the doorway let in the fresh air,
and a view of the scenery. Through a deep ravine, the train
plunged into the mountains. This was the first time we saw
a forest of dwarf trees. I noticed odd-shaped hills with goats
and chickens. When I saw people, I knew that those hills
were human dwellings.

In this fashion we traveled through southern Turkey. Without changing trains, we entered Syria. We had a short stop
in Alepo and a long one in Homs. We shook the straw from
our clothing and combed it out of our hair.

Before we boarded military trucks for further transport,
we stayed in a small garden full of flowers. Starved for beauty,
children tried to get some of the flowers. They rushed to bou-
gainvillea plants which were heavy with blooms, and tried
to break off some of the branches. Instead, their hands were
bloodied from the thorns, and the plants were damaged. The
local population viewed us as barbarians.

The military trucks took us through Tripoli; we entered
Lebanon and went to Beirut. Lebanon charmed us with its
scenery. As far as one could see there were orange groves,
gardens, trees, and flowers. We saw mountains above us.
Below, we spied the blue waters of the Mediterranean Sea.
All these experiences were impressed upon our memory. Our
eyes grew wider and wider so as not to miss anything. It
was December 1946, and we had expected winter and snow,
but here we saw nature resplendent in its beauty.

Our trucks reached their destination. We unloaded at the
beach north of Beirut, at an American camp. We would stay
there until we could rent rooms with Lebanese families. We
moved into luxurious tents. Each tent had a cement floor,
electric light, six beds, and a table with chairs. Comparing
this to our previous accommodations, we felt very fortunate.

We all ran from tent to tent to see if everybody was as lucky. The tents were identical. For meals we went to the common kitchen three times a day. In the evening, the youth were invited to an outdoor movie or a dance.

Most of us were exhausted. Ten days in trucks, railroad cars, and trucks had again depleted our energies. At night we fell asleep like boulders, knowing that we wouldn't have to get up or move again.

During one night, we had a terrible storm with drenching rain, lightning, and thunder. The waves of the sea looked treacherous, as if they wanted to engulf us. We felt secure in our tent until strong gusts collapsed its walls. We found ourselves outside in the rain, with the beds overturned. Other people were in the same situation. There were screams and cries all over the camp. We grabbed what we could and looked for shelter in the officers' mess hall. A crowd was there already, so we huddled together and waited for the storm to subside. As the morning came, the only signs of the storm were downed tents and clothing scattered all over the camp. Everybody ran around searching for their belongings. Others reset their tents. Some clothing hung on the electric wires, but there was one person who had lost a bra. It waved triumphantly on the telephone pole out of everybody's reach. Nobody claimed this loss.

CHAPTER NINE

Antoura

Spring awakening,

Nature rushing, flowering,

Forest greening.

After two weeks of sweet laziness, walking on the beach, movies every evening, and carefree living, we went to Antoura. It was a community about fifteen kilometers northeast of Beirut. In Antoura the family of Loutfalla Abinaghli offered us two rooms. His family of four had one bedroom, a small kitchen, and another small room for everything else. It was extremely generous of them, and they must have had a great trust in humanity to accept eight strangers and share their home with them. We were very grateful, thanked them a thousand times, and apologized for the inconvenience.

How were we to deal with two different cultures and no common language? We did our talking with our hands and a few English and French words.

When we arrived, we carried our belongings tied in blankets. Our host family and neighbors looked at us with great curiosity. As our bundles were put down, one of them opened and onions rolled out, and gathered speed. As we ran after them, our landlords' two sons ran with us to catch the deserters. There was laughter and offers of help. That cemented our friendship and helped us to feel welcome.

Most Poles who came to Lebanon lived privately in Arab homes. As families were reunited, they started a normal life.

Inhabitants of Lebanon preferred to be called Lebanese instead of Arabic. They had a very high culture. Most were fluent in Arabic, French, and English. Every village had a school. Every house had electricity and running water. Villages were very clean. There were no beggars. Social services were excellent.

There were many high schools and universities, with local students and students from all over Asia and Africa. Many Polish students, after graduating from high school, attended the American or French universities in Beirut. Lebanon had very few natural resources, so education and banking were their most important industries.

The Lebanese were hospitable, gracious and religious people. In this country of three million, half were Muslim, and the other half were Catholics of the Maronite or Orthodox rites. One could see on every hill either a convent, monastery, or a school. Mosques were mostly in the cities. People respected their neighbors and the country was peaceful.

We lived in Antoura, but our school was in an adjacent community called Zouk-Michael. Our school was about three kilometers away, so every morning we had to get up very early and run. There were no buses. Regardless of the weather, we went to school. Bronica and Mother took care of the house, cooked and cleaned.

Mother knew that our stay in Lebanon was just another stop. She was haunted by worries. What were we going to do? Where should we go? She worried about her family in Poland, wondering if they had survived the war. We wrote a letter addressed to our grandparents to their pre-war address, and mailed it through the Red Cross. We had very little hope of receiving an answer. We simply wrote that we were all right, and healthy, and were looking forward to seeing them some time in the future. Two months after mailing the letter, we still had no reply.

On the way home from school one day with my girl friend, she asked me to stop with her at the post office to find out if she had a letter from her father who was in Italy. Each time she received a letter I was as happy as if the letter were addressed to me. She would read it out loud, then gave me the letter to read. That made both of us very happy. This time I had a surprise: a letter from Poland was addressed to my mother. Grabbing the letter, and in my excitement forgetting my girl friend, I ran home as fast as I could. That was my marathon. Out of breath, I showed the letter to my mother. She held it with trembling hands, slowly read the address, and delayed opening it. She was afraid of what the letter would reveal. Slowly opening it, she handed it back to me and asked me to read it. The letter was written by my mother's youngest sister, Bronka, who had visited us before the war in Martynowka.

My dearest family,

I can't express our astonishment and joy at finding out that all of you are alive and well. Your letter was such a surprise to all of us that we called our neighbors who had to convince us that the letter was real.

When we found out that you were deported, we went to the Russian Embassy in Warsaw everyday and stood in line for hours to find out where they had sent you and to ask them to send you back to us. After one month of this ordeal the Russians told us not to bother them any more because they had no information about you. Our mother didn't believe them and kept sending us in hope that we might find out something. Meanwhile, she started her own campaign. Every day she said a rosary for your health and safe return. While I was reading your letter, she said her rosary again, thankful for the news about you. The war was very difficult and we all suffered much. We still live in the same village and house. Jozef (mother's youngest brother) died in a German concentration camp in Mathouzen. Edward and Michal, the sons of aunt Zandara were shot on the steps of their house the first day of the Warsaw Uprising in 1944. Being educated in Germany, they had many German friends and during the war they were well off working as art dealers. Their mother adored them and since her husband died, they were her whole life. Their death was a terrible tragedy to her. She not only lost her sons, she lost everything she had and became destitute. She lived in a small shack at the outskirts of Warsaw, still wearing her fur coat. She had one cow that was her prized possession. She tended the cow everyday, leading it into pasture. It was a great tragedy to see her in such a state in her old age. Late in the fall in 1946 she was tending her cow. It was a cold and rainy day. She slipped and broke her hip. There was nobody to help her. She laid in the field until she died. Czeslaw (the oldest brother) died after a prolonged illness. Felek, Kazik, and Marcin were killed in Warsaw's Uprising in 1944. Many other cousins and friends perished. I am married now. My husband is a teacher. He fought in the underground. This war turned everything upside down and it will take a long time for everyone to recover.

If this letter reaches you, write some more about your present experiences. Don't dwell on your past so as not to

*hurt yourself or others. Although the war is over, our lives
didn't change much. (From German occupation to Communist rule.)*

*We think of you constantly and send you our prayers
and love.*

Your whole family and friends.

Bronka

My mother's family had shared our letter with other
members, neighbors, and even strangers who marveled at
our survival and credited our grandmother's prayers for our
deliverance.

I finished reading the letter, but I was sure that my mother
heard very little. The news that her parents were still alive,
and that some members of the family were dead was a little
too much to absorb at once. She took the letter, put it on her
lap, and was lost in her thoughts. Later, on several occasions,
I saw Mother reading the letter by herself.

Antoura was a beautiful community. It hugged the southern slope of the mountains with the view of the Bay of Juni.
Red-roofed homes nestled among the orange groves, while
above them were the white mansions of the wealthy. Though
the community was small, it had a high school and a large
university for men, whose students were from all over Asia
and Africa. The town also had a large church, and sometimes
we went there on Sunday, although our church was in Zouk.

Next to Antoura was Zouk-Michael. There was hardly a
house without a Polish family. There were also three Polish
schools: an elementary, a high school, and a vocational school.
Ema, Michalina, and Helena would graduate from vocational
school that year. I was a sophomore, Josephine was in the
sixth grade, and Thad, in fourth. We couldn't have been
happier, and we felt extremely lucky.

As we settled in Lebanon, students who graduated from high school went to Beirut to French and American universities. Young boys, and many of them, went to Egypt to military academy. Our beautiful friend Theresa who had entertained us in Isfahan was Thad's age. She also had a year older brother, Anthony, whom she liked very much. Anthony admired his two older brothers, who were servicemen in Italy. He dreamed of joining them. The only way he could do it was to go to military academy. Theresa was heart broken when he left. One day she packed her things and walked about five kilometers to reach our house. We were surprised to see her alone with her little bundle. After we learned about her sorrow, we were glad she came. She missed Anthony very much and she looked to Thad to fill the void. She stayed with us a whole month.

Zouk also had a Polish bakery, and many stores which catered to Polish people. The Lebanese, just like the Iranians, quickly learned Polish, and used the Polish language extensively.

One young Arab by the name of Hasan, the son of the store owner, often loaded baskets with fruits, vegetables, and other items. These he placed on his donkey and went from house to house selling his goods. His Polish was excellent. He preferred to be called Janek instead of Hasan.

Mother frequently bought oranges and honey from him. One time she was reluctant to buy honey and told Janek: "Last time you sold me molasses instead of honey."

Janek looked embarrassed and explained, "I only carry pure honey. It is pure *buz, buz*" (made by bees).

Surrounded by so much beauty and kindness, we grew in confidence and felt a real zest for life. We went to school only five days a week, so every Saturday, or other free day, we went to the beach, climbed the mountains, visited other communities, or went to Beirut. If we could have worked here, we wouldn't have had to worry, but there weren't enough jobs even for the natives. Though jobs were scarce, poor people were taken care of. Beggars were taken to shelters.

Once, a few people came to our house and asked mother for help. They said that they were very poor. We had enough bread, so our mother gave them some. When they left our house, they threw the bread into the bushes. When Josephine saw this, she grabbed a handful of nettle and beat the people on their legs. She also screamed at them in Arabic for throwing bread away. They had expected money instead of bread. We didn't have poor visitors anymore.

The wives of soldiers and their families received a small stipend. In our family only Bronica qualified. The grant she received was sufficient to pay her rent, buy food, and some very modest clothes. The rest of the refugees were under the protection of the IRO (International Refugee Organization). Our grant was modest, but we were grateful for it. It paid our rent and food. If we wanted to buy some clothes, they had to be purchased from our food money. Our main staples were bread and lentils prepared in a thousand different ways. Sometimes, we treated ourselves on Sunday with white bread and butter, and hot cocoa. Apparently the food we ate was very healthful, because we all looked well and enjoyed good health.

Our landlords didn't treat us as their tenants, but as their friends. There was some difficulty with the language at the beginning, but, while they learned some Polish, we learned some Arabic. Then we could solve the world's problems in our conversations. Josephine and Thad had no difficulty with the Arabic language. After a short time they spoke as well as our landlords' children. Once, they all went on a day-long hike into the mountains. They ate grapes and figs, and drank goat's milk. In the evening, when they came home, they smelled like goats.

Thad became very popular and had many college friends of his sisters' age. On Saturday, Thad's friends would come to visit him, bringing with them some records and a phonograph. With the first sound of music, more friends and girlfriends would arrive. Everybody would dance late into the evening. Often my mother would make tea, our landlady would bring flat bread, and the dancing would continue a few more hours.

Those young men were wonderful. They were university students who came from rich families. They drove expensive cars and wore expensive clothes. Yet, our two rooms didn't offend them. They enjoyed the company of young Polish girls, and danced until they couldn't move any more. They were perfect gentlemen. Our landlady did not object to having so many young people in the house. She would often sit with our mother, and enjoy the music.

Lebanese females seldom participated in public life or public holidays. Even at funerals, females didn't participate. Men cried, prayed, and carried the coffin to the cemetery. Females stayed home.

Slowly we familiarized ourselves with Lebanese customs and practiced them when the occasion presented itself. *Salam alaikum* — peace be with you, *gif-halik* — good morning, were not enough to great a friend. It was polite to ask about the health of family members, how things were going, and to wish them happiness for the day. Also, one couldn't forget to invoke *Inshallah* — God's protection.

Lebanon was a classroom of ancient history. There were old Roman ruins at Biblos, and the cedars of Lebanon in Baalbek, which had been standing at the time of the birth of Christ. We visited Bikwaya where there was a monastery

1943: In our best clothes
Top row: Michalina, Mother, Helena
Bottom: Gryzelda, Thad, Josephine

1944 – Isfahan
Lala, Gryzelda
and Marysia

1944 – Isfahan
Josephine, Mama, and Thad

1947 – Gryzelda

1946: Antoura, Lebanon – The Niziol family together
Top row: Michalina, Bronica, Mother, Ema, Helena
Bottom: Thad, Josephine, and Gryzelda

founded by a Polish priest who had left Poland after the January uprising in 1863. This monastery had never been visited by females. We were the first group of females allowed inside it. We found many souvenirs from nineteenth-century Poland.

We also met two young Polish clerics there who enjoyed talking to us in Polish. Also, we were surprised and overjoyed to see Father Leon there from Julfa, Iran. Surrounding him, we bombarded him with questions. He told us that he had missed us very much, adding: "Julfa was terribly quiet, and looked empty. I missed hearing you sing in the church. Sing some songs for me."

We liked Father Leon very much. We wanted to sing our hearts out for him. He said: "This monastery is only a short stop on my way to Poland."

What a great human being! We left Bikwaya with tears in our eyes and heavy hearts. We wished we could go with him, but he was not going to our Poland.

On our way home we stopped in Damascus, the capital of Syria and the oldest continuously inhabited city. Our next stop was Zahle, the most modern resort, and the playground of the rich from the Middle East. The prices were out of our reach. We couldn't afford even an ice cream cone, so we admired the beautiful gardens, gorgeous fountains, and hotels, and left the place full of dreams.

Our next stop was Ghazir, where in one of the monasteries our greatest poet, Juliusz Slowacki, spent his last years in exile. There is still a copy of his letter to his mother, telling her how lonely he was and how much he missed his native country. His poignant letters to his mother are classics in Polish, poetry full of longing for lost freedom.

Many Polish servicemen from Italy, Egypt, and Palestine came to Lebanon to visit their families. Families were reunited after eight years of separation. The fathers and the brothers brought friends. With many young girls, wedding bells soon resounded all over. Bronica's husband had suffered wounds fighting in Italy. After regaining his health he came to Lebanon to visit her. She was very happy. When he arrived, they went to the church in Beirut to have a church wedding. On their return we had a small reception.

It had now been three years since the war had ended. Polish forces left Italy for England, where they would be demobilized. Many of the men wanted their families to follow them to England to start a civilian life. Others, rejecting England, chose Argentina, Brazil, Pakistan, Australia, Canada, and the United States. Many also went to Poland. That was the worst choice, because as they reached Poland, they were promptly arrested and sent to Siberia. Stalin called them traitors, because they had left Russia to fight with the British Eighth Army against the Germans, instead of joining the Russian Army. It didn't matter that England and the Soviet Union were allies. Stalin's logic had its own explanation.

Bronica registered to go to Argentina, but first she had to go to England to join her husband. Her husband agreed to sponsor the whole family, so all of us could get to England also. We left Lebanon right after New Year's Day in 1948. Our landlords didn't want to believe that we were really going. They tried to frighten us by saying that England had shortages of food. They wanted us to stay, and couldn't understand why we had came from Iran and were now going to England. Though we told them how we happened to be in Lebanon, they didn't want to accept our plans. They insisted that we stay. It wasn't our decision to stay or to go. Having no means of support, we had to go.

We had many fond memories of sharing happy and sad occasions with our Arabic friends. Their children played with us all the time, and went with us to the beach and into the mountains. They preferred our bread and we liked their flat bread. We exchanged many other things.

The evening before our departure, the whole family came to say goodbye. Our landlord cried, but his wife joked and was in the best of spirits. Next day, he took us to Zouk where we were to take a bus to Palestine.

There were many buses in the school yard, and even more people. Natives from Antoura and Zouk were there, too. Girls were crying, leaving their boyfriends behind. Many girls received stationery with addressed envelopes and requests to write. As the buses started, a long cordon of private cars followed them. At a stop in Beirut, we said a final farewell, and off to Palestine we went.

Reaching the border of Palestine, we boarded the English military train which was going to Egypt. Our destination was Alexandria, but since there was a war in Palestine, we had to take a few detours. In El Quantar East we changed to trucks and under a military escort during the night, we crossed the Suez Canal. The trucks stopped at El Quantar West in Egypt, where we lived in tents for a few days.

The camp was large. Civilians mingled with the American military. Music sounded all over the camp. Every evening we saw a movie. Long walks into the desert in the starlight were accompanied by the howls of jackals and hyenas.

The first day, feeling exhausted by the long journey, I fell asleep in the tent. The heat was intense. I was awakened by music from the camp speakers. I had heard it before, but this time it was such a beautiful melody of "Besa me mucho" that I listened with great pleasure. I tried to hold on to this enchanted moment, when suddenly something broke inside me, and my whole life passed before my eyes. It was frightening, and I started to cry, first quietly, then louder and louder. It alarmed my mother. She tried to find out what was bothering me. I couldn't explain it and kept on crying. I cried the rest of the afternoon and most of the night, with short intervals for naps. The morning brought a little relief. My childhood, which I never had, was never to return.

We were on the move again to another camp in Giza. Since there were pyramids nearby it was only natural to visit them. We admired these monuments of ancient architecture and the efforts with which they were built. In the evenings we saw movies and danced outside the tents. The music blasted all over the camp even if you didn't want to listen to it. When we didn't think of our future, it seemed to be such a carefree life.

After two weeks of this vacation, we got on trucks. On a narrow road between rows of palm trees, we went to Port Said. Later we drove to Alexandria, where we boarded the ship that would take us to England. It was an Italian ship, huge and luxurious. There were many English servicemen going home from the colonies.

The loading of the ship took three days. Every evening there were dances, movies, games, and songs. British soldiers were good dancers and wanted to teach us the English language, and an English waltz. Young children explored the decks and tried to touch and see everything. Moon and stars shone on us, promising a better future.

The anchors were lifted, and the decks emptied. Seasickness took its toll. Blessed were those who were not bothered by the sea. At Malta, more British soldiers boarded the ship. Italians in boats brought their silks, jewelry, and other things. They were beautiful, but we could only admire them.

We reached Gibraltar. The ship slowed and the British military band played the British and Polish national anthems. It was to honor General Sikorski, the chief commander of the Polish Military Forces who had been killed in a plane accident over Gibraltar. If only the rocks could tell about the tragedy that happened there a few years ago! We heard rumors that Churchill had made too many promises to General Sikorski that he couldn't keep, so he had ordered the plane's accident. The pilot survived. What would have been the outcome of the war if Sikorski had not been killed? Would there ever have been Yalta?

A severe storm struck the Bay of Biscay on the shore of France. The storm was so bad that we had to put on life jackets and keep them on for the entire night. Again, Providence intervened, and we reached Southampton safely.

1993—Philip Sherwell's report from Cracow on the return to Free Poland of its wartime leader.

Sikorski is laid to rest with kings and heroes

General Wladyslaw Sikorski, leader of the wartime Polish government-in-exile in London, was re-interred yesterday alongside his country's kings in the crypt of Cracow cathedral.

International conspiracy theories and domestic electoral controversies were set aside as the general was interred in the pantheon of Polish patriots in a ceremony attended by President Lech Walesa, Prince Philip and war veterans who fought with British forces against the Nazis.

The general's final journey, from his temporary resting place in rural England, marks another red-letter day in his homeland's post-communist development.

His widow had insisted that General Sikorski's coffin should return only when Poland was again "free and democratic."

Confusion still surrounds his death in Gibraltar in July 1943 when his plane plunged into the Mediterranean just after take-off. While the crash was officially declared an accident, strong rumors remain of a Soviet-inspired plot to sabotage the aircraft because General Sikorski had become an obstacle to the London-Moscow alliance against Hitler.

The timing of his reburial two days before a general election also provoked claims that Mr. Walesa had arranged the event for yesterday to impress the voters. In the face of this criticism, the president abandoned plans to address the ceremony.

With the strain of Chopin filling Cracow's flag-lined cobbled streets, Poles young and old turned out to watch the cortege make its way from the medieval city center to the hilltop cathedral inside the walls of *Wawel Castel*, ancient home of the country's rulers.

There, during an open-air Mass that was relayed to a several thousand strong crowd, Cardinal Glemp, the Polish primate, recalled the life of General Sikorski.

"At stake was free Poland and this is the prize we have in mind when we look back at the heroic life and tragic death of General Sikorski," said Cardinal Glemp.

The importance placed by Britain on the contribution and bravery of Polish soldiers during the 1939-45 War was signaled by the participation of Prince Philip, in the uniform of a field marshal, Admiral Sir Jock Slater, Vice Chief of the Defense Staff, and Mr. Aitken, Minister of State for Defense Procurement.

Polish pilots played a crucial role in the Battle of Britain and their comrades fought with distinction in North Africa and Italy. Many of them attended yesterday wearing uniforms bearing Polish and British medals.

"We are delighted to be able to honour General Sikorski in our homeland at last," said Professor Wojciech Narebski, in the war and 2nd lieutenant attached to the 8th Army.

"This is the realisation of a dream. He was like our Bethlehem star, the man who guided us in exile. And for many of us he saved our lives by freeing us from the Soviets."

Indeed, in 1941 General Sikorski, Prime Minister of the London-based government and commander-in-chief of the armed forces, secured the release of 200,000 Poles imprisoned by Stalin to form a new Polish army.

But in April 1943 the discovery of the mass graves of Polish officers at Katyn provoked a crisis in his relations with

Photograph: Reuters/Maciej Macierzynski/Archive Photos

**Prince Philip and Polish President Lech Walesa
during the ceremony for General Wladyslaw Sikorski
at the Royal Wawel Castle in Krakow.**

Moscow at a time when Britain and the Soviet Union were close allies.

Three months later the general was killed in the Gibraltar air crash, prompting speculation which has lasted to this day. The reported presence in the colony at that time of Kim Philby, the British intelligence agent who was feeding secrets to Moscow, has served to heighten suspicions of sabotage.

Following a Requiem Mass in Westminster Cathedral, the general was buried at the Polish air force cemetery in Newark, Notts. He was returned to Poland earlier this week at the request of Mr. Walesa.

Across Eastern Europe, reburials are in vogue as countries seeking to re-establish social identities after the destructive years of communism have made efforts to turn their minds to earlier leaders.

But unlike General Sikorski, many have been tainted by their co-operation with the Nazis, such as Admiral Miklos Horthy, the recently reinterred wartime leader of Hungary.

CHAPTER TEN

England

Cold, dampness, shortages,
Struggle, growing, frustration,
Ship on waves afar.

W e were under the impression that, once we reached England, we would find a house and work right away. That "right away" became a reality only after three months. Meanwhile, we moved all over England from one transitory camp to another. In some camps we stayed overnight, in others, a few days or weeks.

We traveled from camp to camp by train, with all our bundles. English people were surprised and annoyed to see such an invasion of unwanted foreigners. They didn't have enough food for themselves, and there were shortages of housing, and yet, they had to share everything with those strange foreigners. They resented our intrusion on their English conservatism. England had lost almost all of its colonies, and Britons were returning home in droves. In this chaos, the newspapers, not so subtly, encouraged foreigners to go home.

We didn't live in tents anymore. Those transitory camps

had previously housed American servicemen. Barracks were constructed from corrugated metal in the shape of half a barrel cut lengthwise. The floors were of blacktop. One or two round metal stoves were in each barrack. We used coal for fuel.

The change of temperature and climate made us extremely miserable. We shivered from cold and dampness. We didn't have winter clothes, and food was rationed. Hundreds and hundreds of young Polish soldiers waited to be discharged and resettled. We were comforted by their sharing of our misery.

We saw an occasional movies, but dances were everybody's favorite. It was the best way to keep warm and to find a boyfriend. The girls who had left their boyfriends in Lebanon had to forget them. Lack of jobs, housing, and food were not the subjects they wanted to write about in their letters. Very often they didn't have money for postage.

Even the most enjoyable things can become burdens. We were worn out by our gypsy life. We wanted to settle down, get jobs, and take care of our needs. Finally, we reached our last transit camp. We were to stay there until something more permanent was found.

Bronica had arrived in England ahead of us. With her husband, she lived in a camp near Cambridge. This camp was changed into a residential community to accommodate discharged servicemen and their families. After they found a barrack-house for us, Bruno arrived with tickets to take us there.

We settled down, and my sisters started looking for jobs. Since there was such an influx of new-comers, the jobs available to us were the ones that English people didn't want. Our professionals and educators worked as dishwashers, swept the underground, and worked in ice cream or jam factories, doing what they could to keep employed.

Ema, Michalina, and Helena found jobs in different

hotels and had to live there. Mother worked in a jam factory. Josephine and I went to school in different parts of England, so Thad was the only one left with Mother. By the fall, Thad went to Rugby, to a vocational-technical school, Ema got married, and our mother was left alone.

Her postponed depression returned. She cried a lot and tried to persuade each one of us to go back with her to Poland. She wanted to mend her broken nest. She thought if we went to Poland, we'd all be together. None of us thought that it was such a good idea. The letters from Poland told about the Communist persecutions, extreme shortages of food and housing, and frequent deportations to Siberia. As much as we would have liked to obey Mother, common sense told us otherwise.

Soon Michalina got married, and Bronica had a son. Josephine decided not to return to school. Difficulty with the English language was too great for her to overcome quickly. When she moved in with her mother, both of them worked in the jam factory. Helena quit her hotel job and joined Josephine and Mother. All these changes focused mother's attention and energies on her new grandson. Soon, Ema with her husband, and Michalina with her husband, moved nearby, so once again Mother had many of us around.

It was a sad day when Bronica left for Argentina with her husband and son. Bruno had suffered wounds during the war and wanted to get as far away from Europe as possible. They promised that after they were settled down and doing well, they would send for us. We lost all hope of ever seeing them again.

I attended Stowell Park, the Polish High School, near Cheltenham, west of Oxford. Once it had been an American military camp. Now those barracks were changed into a dormitory with double bedrooms housing four hundred high school girls. They came from Lebanon, Italy, France, Africa, Poland, and England. They were Polish girls who had come to England to join their fathers.

Although this was a Polish school, all subjects except the Polish language, religion, and history were in English. Those students who had lived in England during the war did the best. I had a terrible problem with English, but I was determined to persevere. Our teachers had the same problem. While learning the language themselves, they had to teach subjects in English.

We adored our Polish language teacher. She was not only a good teacher, but also a highly educated and caring person. She had come to England from a German concentration camp, and still looked like a skeleton. She tried to conceal the number tattooed on her forearm. She treated us like her own children.

Every Saturday she gave a tea party in her bedroom for a small group of students. During the party, she gave us a concert of classical music, playing records of Chopin, Schubert, and other composers. We looked forward to those evenings and felt privileged to be invited. Those evenings were very pleasant and memorable, as well as educational. She always told us something about the composer, explained his music, compared him with other composers, and invited questions. We learned more during those evenings than in the regular classrooms.

The school year 1949/50 ended my high school education. I faced the same question every student did: what do I do next? With my finances, college was out of the question. It was great to make plans when one's pockets were full. My choice was simple: find a job quickly. But where? Should I join my mother in the jam factory or look for something else? Though we had been taught many things, I didn't think I was proficient in anything I could call a profession. Meanwhile, Helena and Josephine left the jam factory and found a job in a store on the American base.

A girlfriend of mine, whose married brother lived in London, tried to persuade me to go with her there and look for a job. I liked her plan, even though I didn't know anybody in London, but I didn't have any money. Not about to give up, my friend promised to help me if I went. There must have been some void in my brain, and I agreed. Since this was vacation time, we both went home to our families and agreed to meet in London in September.

During the vacation I picked fruit, earned a few pounds, and felt rich and hopeful. After buying a few things, with five pounds in my hands I went to conquer London.

We met at the assigned point and time, and had to find a place to stay that night. We found a "bed and breakfast" that cost us one pound each. The next day we looked for a room to rent, and jobs. We found a room for one pound each a week, and the landlady wanted us to pay for two weeks at once. We still didn't have a job, and I had only two pounds left.

Whenever we mentioned that we were looking for a job, we were told to go to the sewing factory, where we could make more money. We went from one factory to another without any success. I didn't know why we wanted to work in the sewing factory. Our knowledge of sewing was limited to threading a needle, sewing buttons, and taking up a hem, but we thought the ability to sew was innate. We had more courage than brains.

Oranges and tomatoes were the only food we could afford. This was what we ate for two weeks. Europe and Israel flooded England with fruits and vegetables, but English people were very loyal to English products despite their inferior quality. They didn't buy anything foreign, so fortunately for us, the prices fell.

I was the first to find a job. As a general helper in a sewing factory, I did everything with great diligence. I also tried to learn how to operate a sewing machine. The day after I was hired, my girlfriend, found a similar job. Finally we felt secure.

Every day, during lunch time, when everybody left, I took scraps of fabric and practiced on a sewing machine. In time I became passably good. With my first pay I paid off my debts. With my steady income, I felt I could do anything I wanted. I bought myself a pair of shoes, a coat, and a dress. These were the very first clothes I had bought for myself in my life. Until now, all my clothes had been hand-me-downs, or things donated by an organization. I even enrolled in an evening school to learn more English.

English people were very reserved. They never started a conversation in public. If a foreigner started it, they cut it short. London was the worst place to learn English. Foreigners, mostly Polish, were everywhere: in workplaces, subways, on the streets, in the stores, restaurants, theaters, and churches. The institutions of learning were full of Polish servicemen and civilians.

Every patriotic holiday was celebrated according to military tradition. Poles participated in every celebration. Those who stayed in England hoped that, some day, they would return to Poland.

I could never afford restaurants or a theater, so on weekends, with a small group of friends, I rode the London subway. We crisscrossed the entire city of London many times. In this way we visited every museum, library, every square, park, and monument.

In 1950 there was a "Great British Exhibition" in London.

This was an exhibit to demonstrate the development of technology in the last fifty years. People were starved for new experiences. It was high time to forget the war, and the past, and to concentrate on the future. Every Londoner took it upon himself to contribute something to the success of the Exhibition. Streets were swept, rubble was removed, and all corners and subway entrances were full of flowers. Bands played in the parks, and people smiled more often. Even nature cooperated: there were fewer rains and the sun shone more often. It was a time of celebration, and people enjoyed it.

The main exhibit, at Sloane Square, became a favorite spot for young people. On Sundays, the symphony orchestra played requests from the public. I went there to listen to the music. The orchestra was good. Music filled the air. One young, beautiful Hungarian lady requested that the orchestra play Brahms' "Hungarian Dances." They played with such spirit that the public asked for encores. I wanted to ask them to play Chopin's "Krakowiak," but I guess I was not aggressive enough. Somebody always shouted his request first. I was discouraged but imagined the orchestra playing "Krakowiak," anyway.

My first year in London went very fast. My school girlfriend had come to England from Africa. Some of her friends lived in London. One Sunday I went with her to visit one of her friends who lived in a three-story house where she cleaned and cooked for seven other Polish tenants.

We had a wonderful time, laughed a lot, and probably made too much noise. This noise intrigued our hostess's brother, who was studying upstairs. He came down to investigate and scolded us for interfering with his studies. We became quiet. Eugene was his name. He didn't go back to his books, but stayed with us. Later he offered to take the three of us to the movies. We considered it a truce offering and gladly accepted. This was a memorable evening. A week later Eugene asked me for a date. I wasn't sure he meant me alone, so I asked my girlfriend to go with us.

One day, my roommate told me that over the weekend she would visit her parents who lived south of London. Then Eugene called, saying: "I have some free time. Can we go to the movies on Saturday?"

I said, "It will be great. Why don't we have dinner here first? I will do the cooking."

I spent all Saturday morning at *Porto Bello*, the Italian market, looking for something to cook. The food was rationed, and my finances were limited. I managed to buy a pound of ground meat, some potatoes and pickles. I made little patties and peeled the potatoes. Fortunately, I didn't have to do anything to the pickles. All I had was a frying pan, a small pot, two cups, two plates, two knives, and a spoon. I used my frying pan to make jelly, and this presented a problem, because now I couldn't fry the meat.

Eugene came around four. I greeted him wearing my apron and hoped that my first dinner would be a success. The potatoes were boiling, but the meat had to wait for the frying pan.

"Why don't we eat the jelly first? Who said that dessert should be last?" said Eugene.

"What a great idea!"

We ate the jelly. I washed the frying pan and fried the patties. I felt that I had cooked a good dinner. But when I looked at the potatoes, they were black. I tasted them, and they were edible, so we ate the meat patties with black potatoes and pickles. After this colorful dinner we went to a movie.

Eugene must have been impressed by my culinary talents. One year later, on September 1, 1951, I became Mrs. Eugene

Lachocki. My husband Eugene, with an engineering diploma in his hand, applied for a visa to the United States.

Our wedding, in the camp where my mother lived, was very modest. Only a few of Eugene's friends and our families were present. Eugene's friends from London gave us a most beautiful wedding present. They gave us a two-week trip to Paris.

By the evening of the next day we were in Paris. We were shocked. In comparison to Paris, London was a poor relative. London was still trying to erase the signs of war. Paris was intact. Food in England was rationed. Paris stores were overflowing with goods. People had beautiful clothes. The crowded restaurants and theaters were noisy.

We found a restaurant near our hotel where the food was exquisite. At our wedding reception we had less food for twenty-five guests than what we had for the two of us in one meal. Our stomachs, accustomed to very small portions, were filled very quickly. We were sorry to leave so much food on the table. During those two weeks we visited the whole of Paris, mostly on foot, and sometimes by Metro. On our return to London, we continued working and preparing for a new chapter in our lives.

We lived in a three-story house owned by my husband's friend and superior officer who was presently a supervisor at work. He lived in the same building and rented out other rooms to his friends. We rented one room on the third floor and could use the kitchen, dining room, and bath on the first floor.

The house didn't have central heating. Each room had a little electric heater. The house was always cold and damp. Later the house was empty, except for us, because it had been sold. Since we were going overseas before the deal could be closed, the previous owner allowed us to stay.

One particularly cold day, it snowed, and I felt miserable. To save electricity, we usually turned the heater off in our room during the day and back on in the evening. This time I decided to keep the heater on during the day.

In the early afternoon I went out to do some laundry, but left the heater on and closed the door so it would be warm when I returned. After doing all my errands I came home and stayed in the kitchen. It was about time for Eugene to come home, so I started cooking on the gas stove. It was getting dark, so I turned on the switch, but the electricity was off. I thought that maybe the bulb needed to be changed. Since everything was cooking, I stayed in the kitchen.

My husband was surprised to find the house in darkness. He checked the fuses and found some of them blown out. When he reached our room, he screamed that there was a fire, and for me to bring a pail of water. I carried it to the third floor. He poured it under our door and then opened it. Smoke engulfed him. There was a little sink under the window in the room so, by touch, and by staying as close to the wall as he could, he reached it and started dousing the fire with water. We couldn't call the fire department because the nearest telephone was two blocks away in an Underground station, and the fire was intense.

I ran down and returned with the largest pot I could find. Both of us poured water on the fire. When we couldn't see any more flames, Eugene opened the window to get some fresh air, and by flashlight we assessed our damages and the damage to the house. Everything we had was charred. The only unharmed items were the clothes we wore and what I had laundered that afternoon. Now we could travel light.

The walls were black; the bed, one scorched mass. The floor had burned all the way through to the second floor ceiling. In addition, the water we had poured on ruined the ceilings and walls on the second floor.

I do not know how my husband had avoided falling through the floor. There were only about two feet of flooring intact near the wall. How he managed to find this supporting floor to get to the sink remains a mystery.

I was emotionally devastated and guilt-ridden. Why had I been so cold, why did I have the heater on, why did I take so long to do my laundry? I couldn't explain any of this. It made me even more guilty when I thought that I could have lost my husband. How could we explain to the owner what had happened? The next day we had to find another room, gather what was left, and move out.

The thing I remember most about the fire was the possibility of Eugene's death, and the tremendous guilt of not being cautious enough to prevent the fire. Since then every time I smell smoke, I think of that event.

Eugene's younger brother, who was in the Merchant Marines, was the first one in his family to immigrate to the United States. On Christmas, 1951, Eugene's parents left for the States. Finally, it was our turn, and on February 26, 1952, on a Greek ship called *Neptunia*, we left from Southampton for Hoboken, New Jersey, via Halifax. The ship was very old. I think only our prayers kept it together. In Halifax the crew had to chop ice from the decks to lighten the load. A year later *Neptunia* sunk during a storm. My sister Ema also came to the United States with her husband and a small daughter at this time. They settled in Chicago.

CHAPTER ELEVEN

Starting Again

Wings spread, breath of air,
Morning, tranquillity, old age,
Courage, hope, new life.

The first few weeks in the United States we spent in total bewilderment. The tempo of life was much too fast for us. The stores were overflowing with goods, low prices, and abundant food. The seven years for Eugene, and four years for me, in England with its quieter tempo had greatly affected us. Here, there were fast, noisy cars, and people everywhere twenty-four hours a day. Stores opened late into the night. It appeared that sleep was of little importance. England went to sleep at eleven. This constant noise in American cities bothered us very much. Eventually, we learned to tolerate it.

We started to look for work right away. It was fortunate for us that Eugene's parents had an apartment and already worked. We stayed with them for two weeks while we both looked for jobs.

It was a difficult time at first. Eugene expected to find a job as an engineer. It was during the Korean War, and factories had government contracts. They didn't want to hire non-U.S. citizens. After an intensive search, Eugene found a job in a small factory as a radio trouble-shooter for $1.25 an hour. We felt fortunate and moved to Newark, New Jersey, where I also found a job in a dress factory filling out orders for stores for $0.80 an hour. With these modest earnings we could pay for rent, for food, and even save some.

By the end of 1952, my sister Helena came to the United States and lived with us. Eugene advanced very quickly. When the Korean War ended, he found a job in a large factory as a junior engineer. Meanwhile, I went to a vocational school to learn bookkeeping. I worked in this profession for the next ten years. Our combined earnings were enough to buy a house in East Orange, and a car. What a luxury! After thirteen years of barracks, tents, stables, and barracks again, to have a house! Only those who had had similar experiences could understand.

Now we understood the meaning of an "American Dream." We not only could have everything we needed and wanted when we worked, but we could also be anybody we wanted to be.

In 1953 my sister Helena married Eugene's brother, Dezi. We liked to keep everything good in the family. They moved to Paterson and we visited each other very often. I also kept in touch with Bronica in Argentina. She had a baby daughter and wrote that life was very difficult.

We became US citizens in 1957 and felt privileged to be members of such a great nation. America is a country of all nationalities. It belongs to people who love freedom, not to a race of people called Americans. There was freedom to do and go where one wanted, whenever one wanted. We took advantage of our new privileges by traveling extensively all over the United States, Canada, and the Caribbean Islands. With citizenship, Eugene could get any job he wanted.

We had many friends and visited our old friends who came from England, Lebanon, and Africa. We tried to keep company with people who were more interested in our future than in our past. We tried to forget the past.

In 1958, Josephine and Thad came to the United States and stayed with us. Josephine found work right away, but Thad had difficulties. Although he was a good mechanic, he was of military drafting age, so no one wanted to give him a responsible job. After six months of this uncertainty, he enlisted in the army, and was promised that he would be sent wherever he wanted to go. Thad wanted to go to England or to Germany, so he could be closer to our mother who was still in England. After boot camp at Fort Dix in New Jersey, he spent a year in Seoul, Korea. I was glad the Korean War was over.

In 1959 Bronica, with her husband, son, and two daughters, came from Argentina to the United States and stayed with us. They looked terribly haggard. After ten years of hard work in Argentina, they didn't have much to show for it. Spanish people had not shown them much compassion or provided social services. They had suffered from prejudice and ostracism. The unstable economy didn't allow for any savings. The value of money changed frequently. One's economic condition could fluctuate from prosperity to poverty during the same week.

Bronica's children spoke Spanish. The eldest two understood some Polish but couldn't speak it. Once, the youngest one, Regina, came to me and asked for a piece of cake. I didn't understand her, so she repeated it louder. I still didn't understand. The third time, she screamed at me, "You are so big and so stupid." Bronica laughed and translated for me. From this moment on, Regina taught me Spanish, and I taught her Polish. Today, Regina is quite good in Polish, but I have forgotten most of the Spanish.

When Eugene was transferred to Philco Corporation, we moved to Philadelphia. We enjoyed Philadelphia very much. It was a beautiful city with a great cultural heritage. We loved the classical music at the Academy of Music, played by the Philadelphia Symphony Orchestra. There were also many theaters and fine restaurants. It was a very rich and wonderful life.

When Eugene found a job with RCA, Radio Corporation of America, as a senior engineer, we moved back to New Jersey and bought a house, where we lived until retirement. I also enrolled at nearby Glassboro College, where I received an A.A.S. in nursing, then a B.A. in secondary education, and an M.A. in biological sciences. I became a teacher and taught in a high school and later in a junior college.

Eugene was very successful in his job. He worked on the Apollo program, which put the first American on the moon and brought him back safely. Eugene's contribution was in communication. Later, he worked on the Shuttle program and received three U.S. patents. Those were very exciting times, and we felt very proud to be Americans.

During the Easter holiday of 1980, another teacher and I chaperoned a group of students to France. I was excited because Paris reminded me of my honeymoon and two weeks of great happiness. Our students were fluent in French, and our itinerary was well planned. We stayed four days in Paris. I was terribly disappointed. It was not the Paris I remembered. The streets were dirty, food was expensive, the hotels were firetraps, people were brassy and unfriendly, and the service was bad. The students were discouraged and outraged.

After four days in Paris we went to Nantes and took day trips into the country. We visited the chateau on the Loire and tasted the wine which was as sour as vinegar. We visited the city of St. Malo, which had been completely destroyed by Germans. We walked the ramparts and tried to imagine how it had looked before the war. People from all over France donated material to rebuild this historic city.

The high point of our trip was a visit to Mont St. Michelle. The cathedral built in the eleventh century was quite impressive. Its architecture represented Romanesque and Gothic styles. It was a marvel of human faith and dedication to the glory of God.

There were six members of our family in the United States, and we brought our mother to visit us nine times. Every time she came, she stayed for a year. She also went twice to Poland to visit her family. Michalina also came twice and toured from Niagara Falls to Florida.

In 1990 Bronica celebrated her golden wedding anniversary. We were like leaves blown all over the world, but for this great occasion we gathered in North Jersey — except for our mother, who at the age of 89 couldn't travel anymore, and she stayed in England. Bronica's children came from Tennessee, Maryland, and New Jersey. Other sisters came from Illinois, New Jersey, Virginia, and Florida. Michalina came from England. There were also relatives from Connecticut, Spain, Canada, and California.

During this reunion we gathered in church for a morning mass. The mass was very moving. The priest congratulated Bronica and Bruno on their golden wedding anniversary, and recalled the struggles, and the faith which had sustained them through their many years of marriage. After the mass, we held a short reception. This was the first time all of us had been together since 1947. There were many events in our lives we had to catch up on. We reminisced and just enjoyed each other's company. We also felt lucky that we still enjoyed good health, good children, and good grandchildren. We felt blessed to be given so much.

Returning from New Jersey to Florida, we took our English guests with us. We stopped in North Carolina for the night in Josephine's summer house. The house was set between mountains by a lake. We enjoyed boat rides, kayaking, and swimming. Refreshed and rested, we continued our journey.

Our English visitors marveled at the vastness of the United States, the wide roads, rest areas, and, above all, the greenery of the trees and the profusion of flowers. At the welcome center in Florida they refreshed themselves with Florida orange juice, and took a map of Florida as a souvenir.

Michalina concluded that Florida looked like Lebanon. The only thing missing were mountains. Ecstatic about the beaches, our English guests wondered why there were so few people.

We started with the attraction we considered the most important, the Kennedy Space Center. After a bus tour through the center, in IMAX, through the eyes of astronauts, we looked at Italy, the Alps, the Himalayan Mountains, and the Galapagos Islands. One astronaut happened to be around, so it was only natural to have our picture taken with him.

We spent two days in EPCOT, one in Magic Kingdom, one in MGM Studios, and one day in Sea World. The English visitors loved everything and appreciated the opportunity to see so much.

Two weeks in Florida went very fast. Soon it was time to return to New Jersey and England. We stopped again in North Carolina for a few days at Josephine's place and enjoyed her hospitality. Helena arrived with her husband, so we had a great time.

One day after swimming, kayaking, and boat riding, we had a barbecue. In the evening we sat by the lake, reminiscing, and enjoying our good fortunes. Later we talked about Isfahan, Lebanon, England, and our scouting days. We sang some still-remembered songs. Our husbands sang army songs; melodies floated over the lake to be enveloped by the night's mist.

There was no end to the songs. Though it was late at night, we hated to break up, knowing that we might never be together again. There was one song with words something like this:

> We were taken from our homes by force, our enemies wanted to erase our country from the map of the world and destroy us, but we persevered, conquered cold, hunger, and sickness. One day we will return to our homes. All of us will return, whether old or young, to our homes, and our free country.

Just a dream. We are old, and if we return to Poland it would be only for a visit. The young ones have a new country to call their own.

Fifty years had brought tremendous changes not only to our lives, but also to the whole world. The destruction and evil of the Second World War were still keenly felt by our generation. Seldom in the history of humankind had there been such cruelty. The savageness of Germany, Japan, the Soviet Union, and Italy were felt poignantly. The machines of death introduced by the Germans were also used by Italians, Japanese, and Russians. What the Germans did in Europe, Italians did in Ethiopia.

Poland lost ten million people. Both Germany and Russia

1959:
Thad in the U.S. Army, Fort Dix, NJ

1960: United States, first meeting
Left to right: Gryzelda, Josephine, Mother, and Helen

1963: East Orange, NJ – Lachocki and Niziol families
Top: Gryzelda, Frank Lachocki, Helena, Bronica, Dezi, Ema, Gene.
Middle: Josephine, Jadwiga Lachocki with Steven, Chester, Bruno.
Front: Hariet, Helenka, Richard, Robert, and Regina.

destroyed almost all Polish professionals. After stealing everything they could from Poland, the Germans and Russians destroyed the rest. Germans even scraped the top-soil from Polish farms and transported it to Germany. If you ever visit Germany and admire their museums, their stores, and their farms, think about everything they stole. Think about the stolen topsoil, and the ashes of the murdered in concentration camps which were used as fertilizers.

The end of the war didn't end Poland's misery. Our so called ally, Russia, kept Poland under the Communist boot for over forty years. Communist ideology thrived best on poverty and ignorance. After years of exploitation Russia finally had to fail because there was nothing more to exploit.

After coming to the United States, Bronica was very sick and spent some time at a hospital. Her son Robert, thirteen at the time, visited her and pleaded with her to come home because "Father cooks so badly that we all feel like throwing up." She promised to do something about it.

The very day after they came to the United States, Bruno found a job, where he worked until retirement. After high school graduation, Robert enlisted in the air force. He was stationed at Guam for six months. He also graduated from college, got married, and had a daughter and a son. He now lives in South Jersey, working as a computer specialist. His sister Helen, who was born in Buenos Aires, also graduated from college. She married an engineer who was born in Italy. Both of them spent one year in Panama while he was in the army. They traveled extensively while in Panama. With Helen fluent in Spanish, they had no problems. Now they have three sons and live in Tennessee.

Bronica's youngest child, Regina, who was born in Berazategni, Argentina, also graduated from college. She lives in New York and is an aspiring actress.

Ema and her husband, after settling in Chicago, bought a hardware store, where they worked until their retirement. Their hard work gave them a comfortable life. Later, they traveled extensively. Their only daughter graduated from college, has two sons, and works with her husband on computers.

Michalina, who lives in England and takes care of our mother, has two sons and a daughter. Her oldest son, Wieslaw, has a high position as an engineer in British Telecommunication. Very talented, he speaks Polish, English, Latin, French, Russian, and Japanese. He travels all over the world, feeling at home everywhere. He married an Indian lady. With their infant son, they visit India every year. They live in London, England.

Michalina's second son, Henry, graduated from college. He married a Scottish lady, who is an artist. She is a very successful painter. They have their own business and are well off. They have one daughter.

Michalina's daughter, Kristina, graduated from college with a teaching certificate. She married a Scotsman. They have a daughter who at four is fluent in Polish and English, and also an infant son. Everyday Kristina takes the little ones to see her mother, who loves to spoil them.

Helena, who married Eugene's brother, has three sons. The oldest son, Richard, after marrying, established a restaurant business in North Carolina. The middle son, Stephen, is married, and has a son and a daughter. He is a master boat mechanic. They live in Pennsylvania. The youngest son, Tom, has a Ph.D. in chemistry. He lives and works in Atlanta. As a freshman, he studied chemistry at the University of Maria Curie Sklodowska in Lublin, Poland. While in Europe, he visited Greece, Czechoslovakia, Austria, Italy, and France. He is married and has two sons.

My husband Eugene had been deported to Russia in April 1940 with his family. After his father was arrested by NKVD (Peoples Commissariat of Internal Affairs), Eugene became head of the family with all the responsibilities. The family spent two years in Kazakhstan in a labor camp. With the amnesty, he joined the Polish Forces. With them he went through Iraq, Palestine, Egypt, and Italy where he fought at Monte Cassino and in other battles. After the war, he studied in Fermo, Italy, and in London. That was where our paths crossed.

Josephine married a Polish engineer. They live in Virginia and have an adopted daughter. Josephine lived in New York for a while, where she attended junior college. She works as a computer operator for Virginia Power.

Josephine has traveled extensively. In 1962 she went back to Lebanon for a visit. All our Lebanese friends were happy to see her and wanted to know everything about everybody. She also visited Switzerland, France, Argentina, Brazil, and Venezuela. She also went back to England, and twice to Poland. Both she and her husband like to travel. Every year they go on a cruise.

Thad managed to finish technical-mechanical school in Rugby, England. After his military service in the United States, he found a good job in South Jersey, where he now lives with his wife and one of his four daughters.

When our family gets together it is like a small United Nations. We can communicate in nine languages. China is the only country none of us has visited.

The Polish refugees of the Second World War brought with them many experiences to their new countries, and worked hard to make a good life for themselves. They became loyal to the new countries but were still curious about what was happening back "home."

We felt good in the United States where so many people had foreign roots. Here, opportunities seemed unlimited. Everybody could try to achieve their full potential. In United States the minute you step on its ground, you feel the promise of a free country.

I visited Poland in 1984 and was very disappointed. It looked more like Russia. There were long lines at every store. I had to report to the police wherever I went. While staying in the hotel overnight, I had to give up my passport to the clerk. What a frightening experience! Everybody wanted dollars without giving anything in return. The people were gloomy and shabbily dressed.

There were huge billboards along the roads with ugly Communist slogans. Warsaw was dirty and sooty, a city with very monotonous, drab buildings. Empty stores were everywhere.

I stopped at the square which was dedicated as a monument to a Jewish Ghetto. The square was empty, as were the emotions of those who had survived the German onslaught. It was an ugly, mournful scene, sad and depressing.

In the middle of Warsaw, in front of the security building, stood a huge statue of the bloody chief of NKVD, Dzierzynski. The pedestal on which the statue rested was about six feet high. He had murdered many Polish people, including children. The Warsawians took it upon themselves to show his guilt in slaughtering so many, by painting the hands of the statue with red paint. The next morning the statue was washed clean, but in the night the students painted the hands again with red paint. Though this occurred in front of the NKVD building, they were unable to catch the culprits.

I also visited Torun, the birthplace of Copernicus. The beautiful cathedral of Torun was used as a prison by the Germans, and as a storage plant by the Communists. The park in Torun was used by Germans as a shooting range to practice their skills on arrested Poles. Next was Poznan. It was as gloomy as Warsaw, except that Warsaw was completely destroyed. Poznan was intact. Germany put Poland back into the nineteenth century.

Zakopane is a lovely resort town in the Carpathian Mountains. Lenin lived here when writing his Communist Manifesto. I also visited the lake, *Morskie Okio* — The Eye of the Sea. To protect it from pollution, traffic is limited. No car can come closer to the lake than ten kilometers. You have to walk the rest of the way, or rent a horse-driven wagon.

I stopped at Czestochowa to pray at the foot of the miraculous picture of the Black Madonna. The church was built in the thirteenth century, and soon became the object of pilgrimages to its miraculous picture. People came throughout the centuries bringing offerings of gold, silver, jewels, amber, crutches, canes, and other things. The treasury under the church had so many priceless artifacts, gold and silver, that Poland could have paid its national debt twice over. However, the government's debt was not the church's debt. Even if the church had offered to pay the bill, the Communists would have stolen the treasure, stayed on, and tormented the people. This treasure was hidden by private citizens during the war. After the war, every single piece was returned to the church's coffers.

I stopped at Krakow, the old capital of Poland. Krakow dates from the Middle Ages and has the second oldest university in Europe. One of its most distinguished alumni was Nicholas Copernicus.

Wieliczka lies at the foot of the Carpathian Mountains, where there is a salt mine dating to the ninth century. It has stayed in continuous use. With a touring group, I went down to the level of ninety-five meters and visited many chambers. Some were made into museums with salt statues depicting many legends of the salt miners. There were also a few small chapels with seats made from the salt.

Salt comes in two colors: gray and green. The floor and columns were made from the green salt, and they looked like marble. The seats, statues, and chandeliers were made from the gray salt. These contrasts presented a beautiful picture. There were also two museums with artifacts from the beginning of the salt mine.

Later we descended to one hundred and thirty-five meters. There were two large lakes, where the concentration of salt in the water was 42 percent. One could take a short ride on a raft. In one chapel, large enough to accommodate 800 people, all the salt statues were carved in a Gothic style. Every Christmas miners, with their families, attended the Christmas Eve Mass there.

Next to the chapel was a large cavern which was used for children sick with pulmonary diseases. During the war the Germans cemented the floor in this cavern and brought prisoners from Auschwitz to assemble the German planes. They turned the chapel into a workshop. Leave it to Germans. They didn't believe in empty spaces. As we walked through the salt mine, we covered four kilometers and it took us two hours.

Not far from the salt mine is the infamous monument to German culture: the Auschwitz concentration camp. I stopped there to remember the bestiality and the crimes committed against humanity. The horror of the place can never be adequately described. I would like every German child to know the deeds of their fathers.

My visit to Poland was very painful. I was born in Poland, but during this visit the Polish authorities tried to convince me that I had been born in Russia. They suggested that upon my return to the United States, I should straighten out my birthplace on my passport. A useless suggestion.

The purpose of my visit to Poland was to visit the place of my mother's birth, and to get to know my living uncles and aunts. The place was a small village named Janowo on the outskirts of Warsaw. My aunt still lived in the house where my mother was born.

The first thing I did was to visit the cemetery where my grandparents and many other relatives were buried. Next, my aunt took me around the village, and showed me big gardens full of raspberries and extensive fields of grain. I was impressed with this abundance and questioned the shortage of food in the stores.

What she told me, I didn't want to hear. She said that these were the fields of death. At the beginning of the war these fields were covered with Polish casualties. Then, the Germans killed Russians. The Russians killed Germans and Poles. She said that at one time, as far as one cold see, there were dead German and Russian soldiers. The Germans routed all the villagers and ordered them to bury the dead. She had to do that too. She was only twenty-eight years old. It took them a whole month to bury the dead on those fields. She said the stench was so bad that even now, almost forty years after the end of the war, the air was still filled with it.

Neither Germany nor Russia removed the remains of their soldiers after the war, so farmers plowed the fields and sowed grain. Though the harvest of grain and raspberries was plentiful, everything was sold to Germany and Denmark. The local population didn't want to touch it.

Poles witnessed too much unpunished crime. Victims were not recompensed for their loss and suffering, while the criminals prospered. I returned to America sad and depressed.

Eugene never went back to Poland and does not intend to. He wants to remember Poland the way he left it.

Now, both retired, we live in Florida and often reminisce about our past. The results of our work gave us a comfortable life. Often, members of our families visit us or we go and visit them. We have many acquaintances, but only a handful of friends. Our experiences didn't make us very outgoing. We enjoy a quiet life. Eugene and I both love classical music, reading, walking, and swimming. Eugene became an amateur radio operator and has found much pleasure in this hobby. I teach in a junior college, and that keeps me busy. I also go to England every year for my mother's birthday. This year she was 91 years old. We enjoy life's simple pleasures, but often ponder our survival. Why is it that in the turmoil of the Second World War we were spared, while millions of others perished? That our lives were miraculously saved is an understatement. I hope we didn't exhaust our quota of miracles.

CHAPTER TWELVE

Ashes to Ashes

Ashes to ashes,
Loving family and friends,
Life's rewards, farewell.

I t was not even a year after Bronica's golden wedding anniversary that most of us gathered again, but this time it was a sad occasion. Bronica's husband had died of cancer.

Death is rarely expected; it always sneaks up on us when we least expect it. Up until this time we had not considered ourselves as senior citizens, but now, sadly, we had to consider this reality. Bruno had never complained. He was always too busy.

When he married Bronica, he assumed responsibility for the entire family. All of us, including Mother, depended on him. He left Archangel only after Bronica was released from prison and the whole family was ready for the transport. While in the army, he checked every arriving train, until he found us. Before he left Russia, he made sure that we would be included in the transport to Iran.

While fighting in Italy at Monte Cassino, he was severely

wounded and spent many months in a hospital. It was a joyous occasion when he came to Lebanon for a visit. Again, he worried about what would happen to us, so he declared all of us as his closest family and with his persistence, we, as a family of a World War Two veteran, were allowed to join him in England. The alternative would have been to go to a Communist Poland.

In Argentina he worked hard to support his family. Even when back pain confined him to a wheel chair, he went to work. Once, during a severe storm, Bruno sat in his wheel chair by his bench and worked with his tools. Lightning struck his work-shop and shook everybody. This electric shock healed Bruno's back. He felt good enough to leave the wheelchair.

When he came to the United States, he worked every day until his retirement at the age of seventy. He had a simple philosophy: if you want something, work for it. He felt that college education was a privilege, and students should pay for it. All his children had a college education for which they themselves paid.

Even when cancer ravaged his body, he seldom complained and went about his business of keeping his yard in good condition. His children espoused his philosophy, and raise their children in the same spirit.

He died the way he had lived, surrounded by a loving family and friends. He was laid to rest in June 1991, in Czestochowa, the Polish cemetery in Doylestown, Pennsylvania.

Two years after Bruno's death, our sister in England, Michalina, lost her husband Stanley to lung cancer. She was devastated. It happened very quickly though the doctors had made rosy promises.

Our mother felt that it was her turn to die. She cried

constantly, asking why she, being old, was spared, while Stanley, thirty years her junior, had died. It is not for us to know. She lost all interest in life. Even her great-grand-children whom she adored, couldn't bring her out of depression.

She had a very good memory until about a month before she died. Then suddenly she couldn't relate to the present time or her family. She went back in her memory to the Russian labor camp. She would wake up in the middle of the night to get ready to go to the factory. She didn't want to be late, she was afraid she would be punished by having her bread withheld. She was having nightmares. One year after Stanley's death, she died of pneumonia. She was 93 years old.

Our family is shrinking. We had all looked forward to retirement hoping to do the things we couldn't do while working. Unfortunately, failing health and lack of energy spoil our dreams. Last year our youngest sister, Josephine, lost her husband. Now three of my sisters are widows. The funerals force us to think about our own end.

Once I heard that the minute we are born, we are destined to die. We were given a long, though difficult life and we have many things to be grateful for.

•~ THE END ~•

G RYZELDA NIZIOL LACHOCKI was born in a small village in the eastern part of Poland, now part of the Belarus Republic. Her family's quiet, bucolic lifestyle was suddenly interrupted in 1939 by the Russian invasion. Her entire family was unceremoniously deported, and they spent two years in a labor camp near Archangel in Northern Siberia. She was educated on four continents, and came to the USA as a young bride. The beginning was rather difficult, but drawing on her experiences in the Siberian labor camp, and refugee camps in Iran and Lebanon, she was well equipped to overcome life's hurdles.

With the support of her husband Eugene, an electronic engineer, she managed to become a bookkeeper and a registered nurse. She obtained her MA in Secondary Education and became a biology teacher. She taught in High School and in Jr. College from which she retired. Now, she lives in Florida with her husband.

The author spends her retirement doing charity work, writing, corresponding with her many friends all over the world, traveling, and reading.

To order additional books, please use coupon below.

Mail or fax to:

Brunswick Publishing Corporation

1386 LAWRENCEVILLE PLANK ROAD
LAWRENCEVILLE, VIRGINIA 23868
Tel: 804-848-3865 • Fax: 804-848-0607
www.brunswickbooks.com

Order Form

❑ *Goodbye Tomorrow* by Gryzelda Niziol Lachocki

$19.95 ea., hardcover .... $ _____

$14.95 ea., paperback .... $ _____

❑ *Niezapomniane Jutro* by Gryzelda Niziol Lachocki

$14.95 ea., paperback .... $ _____

❑ *No Return* by Eugene Lachocki

12.95 ea., paperback .... $ _____

Total, books... $ _____
VA residents add 4.5% sales tax .... $ _____
Shipping – within U.S. and Canada

$4.50 1st copy .... $ _____

$.50 ea. additional copy .... $ _____

Overseas, $9.00 1st copy .... $ _____

$2.00 ea. additional copy .... $ _____

Total .... $ _____

❑ Check enclosed.

❑ Charge to my credit card:

❑ VISA ❑ MasterCard ❑ American Express

Card #_____ Exp. Date _____

Signature: _____

Name _____

Address _____

City_____ State_____ Zip _____

Phone # _____